P9-CMA-874

"I Want You Too Badly To Play Fair,"

Preston said. "So here's your warning, angel. Leave now or stay and pay the consequences."

"What consequences?" Lily asked.

"Gamble with that sweet body of yours."

Lily paled but didn't walk away. He admired her spirit, but wanted to warn her not to let every damned thing she felt show on her face. He should walk away.

Lily stood poised like a rabbit ready to run from a predator. He knew one wrong word would send her flying from him. And he knew that he should be saying that wrong word and sending her away.

But one *right* word would make her stay....

Dear Reader,

Ring in the New Year with the hottest new love stories from Silhouette Desire! *The Redemption of Jefferson Cade* by BJ James is our MAN OF THE MONTH. In this latest installment of MEN OF BELLE TERRE, the youngest Cade overcomes both external and internal obstacles to regain his lost love. And be sure to read the launch book in Desire's first yearlong continuity series, DYNASTIES: THE CONNELLYS. In *Tall, Dark & Royal*, bestselling author Leanne Banks introduces a prominent Chicago family linked to European royals.

Anne Marie Winston offers another winner with *Billionaire Bachelors: Ryan*, a BABY BANK story featuring twin babies. In *The Tycoon's Temptation* by Katherine Garbera, a jaded billionaire discovers the greater rewards of love, while Kristi Gold's *Dr. Dangerous* discovers he's addicted to a certain physical therapist's personal approach to healing in this launch book of Kristi's MARRYING AN M.D. miniseries. And Metsy Hingle bring us *Navy SEAL Dad*, a BACHELORS & BABIES story.

Start the year off right by savoring all six of these passionate, powerful and provocative romances from Silhouette Desire!

Enjoy!

Joan Marlow Golan

Joan Marlow Golan
Senior Editor, Silhouette Desire

Please address questions and book requests to:
Silhouette Reader Service
U.S.: 3010 Walden Ave., P.O. Box 1325, Buffalo, NY 14269
Canadian: P.O. Box 609, Fort Erie, Ont. L2A 5X3

The Tycoon's Temptation

KATHERINE GARBERA

Silhouette

Desire

Published by Silhouette Books

America's Publisher of Contemporary Romance

If you purchased this book without a cover you should be aware that this book is stolen property. It was reported as "unsold and destroyed" to the publisher, and neither the author nor the publisher has received any payment for this "stripped book."

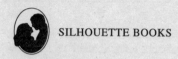

SILHOUETTE BOOKS

ISBN 0-373-76414-6

THE TYCOON'S TEMPTATION

Copyright © 2002 by Katherine Garbera

All rights reserved. Except for use in any review, the reproduction or utilization of this work in whole or in part in any form by any electronic, mechanical or other means, now known or hereafter invented, including xerography, photocopying and recording, or in any information storage or retrieval system, is forbidden without the written permission of the editorial office, Silhouette Books, 300 East 42nd Street, New York, NY 10017 U.S.A.

All characters in this book have no existence outside the imagination of the author and have no relation whatsoever to anyone bearing the same name or names. They are not even distantly inspired by any individual known or unknown to the author, and all incidents are pure invention.

This edition published by arrangement with Harlequin Books S.A.

® and TM are trademarks of Harlequin Books S.A., used under license. Trademarks indicated with ® are registered in the United States Patent and Trademark Office, the Canadian Trade Marks Office and in other countries.

Visit Silhouette at www.eHarlequin.com

Printed in U.S.A.

Books by Katherine Garbera

Silhouette Desire

The Bachelor Next Door #1104
Miranda's Outlaw #1169
Her Baby's Father #1289
Overnight Cinderella #1348
Baby at His Door #1367
Some Kind of Incredible #1395
The Tycoon's Temptation #1414

KATHERINE GARBERA

is a transplanted Florida native who is learning to live in Illinois. She's happily married to the man she met in Fantasyland and spends her days writing, reading and playing with her kids. She is a past recipient of the Georgia Romance Writers Maggie Award.

DEDICATION:

Women friends are important to me, and I wanted to take this moment to say thanks to some of the incredible women who have touched my life.

Nancy Thompson, Francesca Galarraga and Mary Louise Wells: Thanks for being my cheering section, crying shoulder and laughing buddies—in short, my friends. Without you ladies, I don't think I'd be sane!

Linda Beardsley, Donna Sutermesiter and Charlotte Smith: Thanks for always believing in me.

Jude Bradbury and Susan Hartnett: Thanks for giving me a strong example to follow. Thanks somehow seems inadequate, but it will have to do!

And, too, two little ladies who influence me by the example of their joy in life, Courtney Garbera and Katie Beardsley.

ACKNOWLEDGMENT:

A special thank you to Mesty Hingle, who shared her knowledge of New Orleans with me and also some books on her beautiful city. Any mistakes are my own.

One

"**M**r. Dexter will see you now."

Lily Stone gathered her day planner and followed the secretary through the walnut paneled door. New Orleans was hot in the middle of August, and she wished she were outside baking in the sun instead of standing in this nicely air-conditioned room.

She'd wasted at least two days trying to meet with Dexter, and she was determined to stay in his office this afternoon until he met with her.

Her heels sank into the thick carpeting as she walked into the office of the CEO of Dexter Resort & Spa, an international hotel company. The entire room was posh and sleek, decorated with chrome-and-glass furniture and the kind of big desk meant to intimidate whoever sat in the guest chair.

It worked.

Her attaché case felt as if it were made of lead instead of leather. It bumped awkwardly against her leg as she approached the large desk. She'd been successfully running her family's business since she was twenty, but she suddenly felt as if this was her first big client. She wore her best suit, a black-and-red affair that her assistant, Mae, said made her look sharp and professional.

Preston Dexter stood to greet her. He held her hand for the required three pumps and then slid away. His palm had been warm against hers, and his long, neatly manicured fingers had made her hand look small and fragile. Just the way she felt.

He smelled of expensive cologne but also of something essentially male. Not unlike her brothers. The thought helped her relax. It didn't matter that this man could buy her house and business with his pocket change. He was just a guy like Dash and Beau.

Except there was something indefinable about him that made him different from Dash and Beau. She stared at his gray eyes for a moment. There was an element of cold calculation in his eyes. An element of world-weary cynicism that her brothers didn't have.

"Ms. Stone, please have a seat. I'm sorry to have kept you waiting."

She doubted he was really sorry. Probably he regretted that she'd spent the afternoon sitting in his lobby, but she knew they were going to have a problem if they didn't talk now. He'd sent back three of her proposed room enhancements for the regular guest room in White Willow House, and time was running out. The resort would be opening January 1.

Decisions needed to be made and antiques found, then replicated for his newest resort. Her antique shop, Sentimental Journey, did a brisk business of adding finishing touches to many of the older mansions in Louisiana.

"No problem."

She'd been on her own a long time, and she'd never felt so shaken by another person's presence, especially a man. But his gray eyes entranced her. There, hidden in the frozen depths, was something that made her want to reach out to him, the way she had to her brothers when a girl had just rejected them.

He wore his Armani suit with an ease that was out of step with the men she knew. They were all blue jeans and overalls types. Working-class men with cal-lused hands and dirty nails.

"What can I do for you, Ms. Stone?" he asked. He settled back in his executive chair, steepling his fingers across his chest as he waited for her response.

His lips were hard looking, and she wondered if they'd feel firm under her own. The first tingles of de-sire pulsed through her body. Her nipples tightened against the lacy camisole she wore under her suit jacket. Her pulse increased and she shifted restlessly in her chair.

Damn! What was wrong with her? This was a professional meeting. One she'd struggled for a week and a half to have.

Forcing her attention back to her rehearsed speech, she took a calming breath and compelled herself to ignore the desire pulsing through her body, making her heart race and her blood sing. "Thank you for seeing me this afternoon, Mr. Dexter. As I told Mr. Rohr, I like to know the people behind the houses where I place antiques."

"No problem. I'm not planning to keep White Willow House as my home, as you know. It will be the newest in the Dexter Resort & Spa chain."

She crossed her legs and felt the slit in her skirt open. She tugged it back together, uncomfortable showing that much thigh.

"Mr. Rohr mentioned that to me. I want to create an image that fits with the corporate culture of the Dexter chain. Since you sent back the last two proposals I submitted, I thought it would be best if we met face-to-face."

"I can answer all of your questions in about fifteen minutes. I'm afraid I have a dinner meeting across town. I'm still confident that your firm can do an excellent job with the decor."

Lily relaxed as they started talking business. He was a busy man and a little impatient with her for demanding to meet with him. In fact, he'd rescheduled this meeting twice already, but Lily had refused to be put off this time. As the CEO of Dexter, he had an intimate knowledge of the inner workings of the company and its corporate culture, and she wanted the kind of information that couldn't be gleaned from the annual report or a prospectus. She wanted to create more than a hotel lobby decorated with antiques. She wanted to create the warm feeling of home.

She concentrated on staring just over his shoulder so that she wouldn't have to think about the cleft in his chin or the way his eyes seemed to see right through her clothing.

"I like to see the personality of a family or business reflected in the rooms."

"Well, I'll be happy to help. I was impressed with your work on the Seashore Mansion in Hilton Head," he said, smiling at her with the kind of charm that usually annoyed her. He had charisma. Not like Hollywood hotshots that were all flash and no substance, but energy and verve about his business that made him seem alive in a way she'd never been.

"How did you know I decorated the Seashore?" she asked. She'd done the mansion as a favor to her college roommate and her new husband. It had been her first commercial job.

His gray eyes narrowed, focusing on her mouth. Did she have something on it? Oh, damn, her lipstick had probably smeared onto her teeth. Great way to make a first impression!

"The owner is a friend of mine," he said.

She ran her tongue over her teeth hoping to wipe away whatever he'd been staring at. He knew Kelly?

"I spent six weeks down there talking to Brit and

Kelly before I started working on the Seashore. But your timetable is a bit tighter.''

She pulled her day planner out of her attaché and began making notes. The planner made her feel invincible. It was an important tool for staying organized, and she'd written the word *relax* on the top of today's date. She smiled as she read it now. She'd also composed a list of questions, because she'd figured he wouldn't give her the full thirty minutes she'd asked for.

''Well, what would you like to know about Dexter Resorts? We're a family-founded company that has grown since the early twenties.''

''I read the annual report and your prospectus. Tell me about yourself and what you like best when you stay in a hotel.''

His eyes narrowed, and now that her eyes had adjusted to the sun she could see the details of his face. His jaw was square and strong and if she hadn't felt confident about herself and the job she could do, she would have stood up and left.

''What do my likes have to do with the hotel lobby or guest rooms?''

She paused for effect. Obviously Dexter was used to people jumping when he told them to. But then again so was she. ''I can narrow down my list of selections.''

''Buy what Rohr told you to buy,'' he said. His tone was cold.

''If all you want is an inventory list of antiques, Mr. Dexter, maybe you should find another decorator.''

''I want the same quality service you gave the Sea-shore Mansion.''

She smiled at him. ''Well then, I'll need some answers.''

''Did you ask Brit all these questions?'' he asked, one eyebrow coolly raised. So he knew Brit and not Kelly.

''No, I asked Kelly. Do you have a wife?'' The personal question obviously threw him because he sat back in his plush chair and didn't speak for a minute.

''No.''

She doodled on the blank page in her planner. How could she have asked that question?

''I'm sorry. I shouldn't have pried into your personal life. ''

''No problem,'' he said. ''I pushed you. Why didn't you back down?''

For the first time since they'd begun talking, she looked him straight in the eye. Curiosity and a spark of interest that was blatantly male replaced the aloofness.

''Would you?'' she asked, turning the tables on him. There was something about Preston Dexter that made her think if she let him get the upper hand, he'd keep manipulating her.

''No, but I'm used to people jumping when I order them to do so.''

''So am I,'' she said, unable to keep the amusement out of her voice.

Dexter laughed, and for a minute he didn't intimidate

her. There was a hint of vulnerability and mirth on his face. She smiled to herself, knowing that she'd created the kind of bond she always sought with her clients. Laughter went a long way to establishing trust.

"Where did you learn to give orders?" he asked.

"I raised my two younger brothers, and they would run roughshod over anyone who couldn't stand their ground."

She could tell he wanted to ask more questions about her background but he controlled his curiosity and started telling her his likes and dislikes in a resort hotel. He was a sophisticated man, but his tastes were simple.

"I don't want to feel like I'm in a museum and not allowed to touch anything, or that if I sit in some fragile-looking chair it'll fall apart," he said. And Lily felt herself begin to like the cold, hard, sophisticated man behind the desk, and that scared her. Because he seemed like the adventure of a lifetime, and she wasn't the adventurous type.

Preston didn't usually give into the whims of decorators who demanded to see him. He preferred to have that work directed by Jay Rohr, one of his vice-presidents. He trusted Jay's opinion because Preston paid him top dollar. One of the lessons he'd learned at his mother's knee was, you get what you pay for.

When Jay had asked him to meet with the decorator, he'd been annoyed and had agreed reluctantly. Now he was glad he had. He'd expected her to be demanding and pushy. The bossy kind of woman who had manipulated one of his executives into agreeing to have Jay do something he normally wouldn't do.

He hadn't expected to react to her on a male-female level. Every other decorator he'd met at the grand openings of his resorts had been matronly and well coifed. This Lily Stone had a freshness about her that he'd never encountered before. Oh, she was well put together, but there was something about her that didn't mirror the fashionable ladies he'd met with in the past.

Her long, sexy legs made him think of steamy afternoons in bed. Which was totally out of line for a business meeting. He loved that she kept tugging on the hem of her skirt trying to lengthen it.

When she'd walked into the room, she'd projected professionalism, but it had been laced with a genuine goodness he didn't normally see in the world of big business. He made a mental note to research her company. Where had she come from?

Her skin when they'd shaken hands had been soft and gentle. They were a lady's hands, with short practical nails. And he tantalized himself with the imagined feel of her touch on his body. His groin tightened, and he shifted subtly in his big leather chair.

He shouldn't be reacting to her this way, he reminded himself, but she intrigued him.

His office should have intimidated her. He'd seen savvy business professionals lose their cool when entering his private domain. He'd set it up so he'd have the upper hand during any meeting he conducted there.

But it didn't affect her. She'd proven that by the way

she'd stood up to him. It made him want to test her again.

He liked her backbone and self-confidence. He liked the spark in her blue eyes and the way she'd pushed right back at him. Invading areas of privacy that no one else dared, because he paid their salary and they couldn't afford to anger him.

But Ms. Stone didn't seem anxious at all. That fact should have irritated him but didn't. Probably because he was entranced by her body.

She didn't have a fashion model's frame with exaggerated breasts and no hips. Instead she was generously curved, her slim waist accentuated by her suit. Her legs were long and slim encased in black hose, and he wondered how they'd feel wrapped around his waist. What would she do if he asked her to sit on the edge of his desk so that he could stand between those long endless legs and kiss her?

Probably slap him with a sexual harassment suit. And rightly so. But his mind kept supplying images he had no right to be entertaining about this woman.

Her nose was pert and upturned at the end. Her red hair was cut in a short, flattering style that was enchanting with her features. She looked as if she was from another world. One in which he wouldn't have been comfortable living but one he'd like to visit—with her.

He'd had a physical reaction to her from the moment she'd walked in the room and awkwardly bumped her briefcase against her leg. There was something about her show of nerves that hadn't been revealed in her voice, posture or conversation, yet had been betrayed by her body.

The telling motion had given him the advantage he'd needed. Though the room didn't bother her, he did. And he didn't want her bothered in that way. There was a freshness in her face and in her eyes that he'd forgotten existed in the world. And he wanted to make her his woman.

"Well, now I have a better feel of what needs to be done in the lobby, suites and guest rooms. It won't mirror Seashore Mansion in style, but I think your guests will have that same warm feeling," she said, jotting another note down in her day planner.

"I'd really like to create the timelessly elegant feeling that the Van Benthuysen-Elms Mansion has. Have you been there?"

"Yes, several times. What do you like about it?"

Her businesslike tone needled him. His body's reactions to her were leading him into personal territory, and now he had to catch her up. Preston was suddenly glad he'd learned flirting from observing a master—his father.

"Do you have time to stop by there with me? My meeting is being held in the dining room there."

"Now?"

"Yes."

"Let me check my schedule," she said, consulting her day planner again.

"I think I can squeeze you in," she said, a twinkle in her eye.

"Are you teasing me, Ms. Stone?"

"Yes, I am, Mr. Dexter." It had been a long time since anyone had sassed him the way she was. He couldn't remember any business associate behaving that way toward him. He wielded a lot of power in the business world and came from generations of wealth, so others were suitably reserved around him. Not Lily Stone.

"We can continue our discussion in the car."

"What will I do with my car?"

"I'll have one of my employees follow us over, and you can leave from the mansion. What do you drive?"

"My '59 Chevy pickup might be a step down from what any of your employees are used to driving."

"I'll offer him a bonus."

He picked up the phone and called down to the lobby to have his car brought up from the garage and to arrange for one of the security men to follow them in Lily's car.

"It's all arranged, Ms. Stone."

"Call me Lily," she said, her blue eyes sparkling like the waters of the Atlantic.

"I'm Preston," he said with a smile he'd been told was irresistible to women.

"No nicknames?" she asked.

He wasn't sure he liked the way she tried to take control of the conversation. He was the one seducing her, yet he couldn't help but feel a little bit captivated himself. "No."

"Why not?" She asked before he could redirect the conversation.

He tried to think of one person he knew who might call him by a pet name. No one came to mind. He wasn't the type of man who inspired those around him to call him by a sobriquet. Never had been; he'd always been so serious, and intent on making his life a bigger success than his father's. "I'm just not a casual sort of guy around the office."

He stood and picked up his briefcase. Lily shoved her day planner into her attaché and stood, as well. Preston congratulated himself on having brought a close to that line of questioning.

"What about your close friends?" she asked, as they exited his office.

She was losing some of her charm, he thought. He preferred women who looked pretty and said little. She forced him to examine something he didn't really want to—there was a big emptiness in his personal life. Always had been.

"Brit calls me Preston. And I don't have any others who aren't also business associates." Even Brit was a business associate. Preston was a silent partner in the Seashore Mansion.

"That's odd."

"Not really. My work is my life." And he'd learned early on that most people wanted something in exchange for friendship with him—usually money, business advice or social connections.

She pondered that for a minute, worrying her lower lip. Her lips' natural color was a pale pink that reminded him of the roses his mother had always ordered for the breakfast room. Would they taste as soft as those rose petals had felt?

"My business is important to me, too, yet I still have friends away from it," Lily said.

She was charmingly naive to compare her small business to his international corporation. He liked that she didn't fully comprehend the power he wielded in the hospitality industry.

He didn't want to talk about his personal life or the lack of close acquaintances. Instead he wanted to move their conversation back to her. Why had she raised two younger brothers?

"Well, our lifestyles must be different."

She laughed. "I'll say."

He didn't want to like her because he desired her and he knew that emotional entanglements were better left as business transactions.

"I've never met anyone like you."

"Is that good or bad?" she asked.

He realized that seducing Lily would be good for him, because she had the kind of charming innocence that everyone needed to remind them of a better way of life. He knew he was going to seduce her, because for the first time in a long while he felt alive. He looked forward to the challenge of taming the feisty woman.

"I don't know."

The elevator arrived, and they traveled down to the lobby in silence. Joshua, one of his young security men had brought the Jag up and waited for Lily's keys. "We're going to the Van Benthuysen-Elms Mansion on St. Charles."

"Yes, sir."

Lily was busy digging her keys out of her bag. She handed them to Joshua, and he walked away.

"Okay, I'm ready to go," she said.

Preston deftly grasped her elbow and escorted her outside to his waiting car. Even though she was sassy and confident, she might still fall neatly into his hands. It had been a long time since anyone had challenged him on any level. Longer still since a woman had intrigued him on so many.

Two

Lily knew she must have been temporarily insane to agree to ride anywhere with this man. His car had leather seats, a tracking computer that made adjustments to their travel plan, to avoid traffic, and Vivaldi in surround sound. His touch had traveled through her body like lightning through the night sky. A stark, brief illumination and then nothing but the rumble of aftershocks.

She didn't usually react to men she'd just met this quickly. He invigorated her. He also enervated her, making her skin feel too sensitive, her blood race through her veins and her senses sing.

He'd been impatient with her, and she knew he'd meant to brush her off after the first five minutes or so because she'd dealt before with busy executives. They always wanted top quality, yet they didn't necessarily want to invest the time needed to get it.

But an indefinable thing had passed between them. She felt a connection to this man because, despite what she'd told him, her work was her life, as well.

She felt his eyes on her legs as she tried to smooth her skirt down. Never again was she buying a suit without trying it on. His gaze on her legs brought back the insecurities of girlhood.

It was ridiculous, considering she was a mature woman of twenty-five. She ran a successful antique decorating business and had been operating it on her own since her grandmother had retired to Florida a year ago with her longtime love, Humberto.

She couldn't think when he was watching her. All she could think was that his car cost more than Dash and Beau's college tuition together.

"This is some car."

"I know. I had a hand in the design."

"Really?" she asked. Aside from decorating, the only thing she'd ever designed had been the advertisement she'd run in the phone book, and that had been somewhat limited.

"Yes, I gave them a list of items I wanted included."

He sounded like her brothers had when they'd gotten the exact gift they wanted on Christmas morning. She smiled to herself. What was it about men and cars? "I didn't know you could do that. Do American car makers offer that service?''

''I think most of them will if the price is right. Anything's possible if you're willing to pay for it.''

''I take it you are.''

''Haven't you found that things you want the most have the highest price?'' he asked. He glanced over at her as he cruised to a stop for a red light. She studied the intriguing lines around his eyes. He must spend a lot of time outdoors, she realized.

''No, I haven't.''

''Name one thing worthwhile that isn't costly,'' he said.

She hesitated. Once the conversation went down this avenue, there was no going back to being casual business acquaintances. Something in his gray eyes compelled her to speak from the heart. ''Love.''

The light turned green, and he accelerated, leaving the neighboring car in the dust. ''Love is a child's fantasy. Name something real.''

She couldn't believe his attitude. Without love she'd have nothing in her life. Her brothers' and grandmother's affection grounded her. ''Love is real.''

''Sure it is. And so is the Easter Bunny and Santa Claus.''

''Love is more than the holiday traditions, and it encompasses them, as well. It's the warm feeling that comes from knowing you're not alone in the world.''

''Affection.''

''It's deeper than affection.''

"I'll take your word for it."

"Why don't you believe in love?" she asked.

"Because it can't be bought."

She was silent. There was something about Preston that touched her heart. He made her want to fight battles for him, even though he was the kind of man who'd fight and win his own. He made her want to coddle him and shower him with caring, because there was a big cold dark part of his soul visible in those frozen eyes.

As much as she wanted to mother him, she'd been aware of him as a man. She shivered, remembering the narrowing of his eyes and the practiced warmth of his smile.

And there was something prepared about his charm, she realized. Something that wasn't quite genuine. Almost as if he'd learned how to manipulate women a long time ago and no longer had to think about what he was doing.

"Haven't you ever been in love?"

"No. But I've tried lust a time or two. What about you?"

"No to both of them. But I'm sure that my one true love is out there."

"What makes you so sure?"

His voice was dark and deep, sending shivers of awareness through her. She wondered if the attraction she felt toward him was to blame for her reactions. Or maybe it was the fact that for the first time in seven years she was free. She didn't have to be home by nine

to make sure her brothers had completed their home-
work and were getting ready for bed. She didn't have
to hurry back because Grandmother needed to be reminded to take her medication. She didn't have to answer to anyone save herself, and that scared her.

"I'm sure because my parents found each other."

"Maybe their relationship was a fluke."

"Then why do so many people spend their lives trying to capture that feeling?"

"Because they've been brainwashed into believing
in something that doesn't exist. Each generation passes
on the brainwashing so they don't seem foolish."

"Preston."

He raised one eyebrow. "Prove me wrong."

"How?"

He pulled into the parking lot of the mansion, and
the valet attendant came to park the car. Lily didn't
want to stop their conversation but knew she'd have
to. No matter how fascinating she found their discussion, he was still her client and she needed to remember
that.

She was aware that her views weren't necessarily the
views of her peers, but she'd always believed there was
a man out there waiting for her. A man who'd want to
live in New Orleans with her and help her run the business that had been in her family for three generations.
When the bellman opened the door for her, she exited
the car and waited for Preston.

But as she watched Preston pass his keys to the attendant and walk toward her, she forgot all of that.

Because even though he didn't believe in love, Preston Dexter made her pulse race, her skin tingle and her mouth long for the feel of his.

He pulled her into a small enclave outside of the hotel. "Still want to prove that love exists?"

"Yes."

"You find one example of someone who married for love and only for love and I'll give you your heart's desire."

She wondered if he was willing to pay the price she wanted, because her heart's desire might be this dark man with his cynical world view and fallen-angel eyes.

Preston Dexter seemed like an adventure waiting to happen. The male knowledge of intimacy in his eyes sparked an answering need deep within her femininity and promised more excitement than she'd had in her entire lifetime, and that scared her.

But she hadn't spent a lifetime keeping her family business a success and raising two unruly hellions for nothing. "You're on."

Preston asked the hostess to allow them to visit several of the rooms in the mansion. And though she warned it was against policy, she allowed them to tour the house. Preston gave Lily a list of things he liked and pieces he'd love to see her find for White Willow House. They lingered in one of the drawing rooms. The elegant settee was too small for a modern man but just right for the sweet lady who had perched on it to make her notes.

As well as he knew that Lily would be unable to find a couple who'd married for love alone, he kind of wished she would, because he wanted to give her her heart's desire.

"This place is lovely," Lily said.

"Not as lovely as you," he said. He sincerely meant the words. He'd mastered the art of compliments a long time ago and he'd forgotten how to be genuine, but Lily reminded him. She was charmingly naive about things like love and reality but she knew her stuff when it came to antiques and their worth. She'd spoken easily of the Italian sandstone mantels and the imported tapestries.

"Don't say compliments you don't mean. I'm not one of your society girls who'll believe them," she said.

"I never say anything I don't mean."

She walked toward him like an angel in an erotic dream. Her hips swaying in rhythm with the tapping of her heels on the hardwood floor. His pulse picked up the beat, pounding in time to her movement. She moved like sin itself. And though he was a sinner and easily tempted, he knew she'd entice a saint.

The heat of the day lingered in the house but was nothing compared to the fire Lily started in Preston's body. He didn't know where it started, only that it spread to every part of his being like a wild blaze out of control.

Every time she walked into a room he started to harden, and for once he wasn't certain of his self-mastery. She made a mockery of the possession he'd always had over his reactions. He knew why it didn't bother him: he liked the feeling. There was something forbidden about her.

"Don't flirt with me, Preston. I still believe in happily ever after, and once I find that married couple I'm going to make you believe in it, too."

He wished she could, but he knew himself too well. He had learned hard lessons early on. "We'll see, angel."

She bit her bottom lip, and he ached to take it between his teeth and suckle the sweet fruit of her mouth. He wanted to ravish her mouth and learn her taste so completely that he'd always know it. Though she'd gone from sweet to sassy in her conversation, her lips promised all sass and spunk with the honeyed warmth of woman.

She was innocence, where he was jaded realism. She was sweet light, where he was dark shadow. She was the warm feeling of home, where he was the cold luxury of an empty hotel room.

His body hardened in a sudden rush, and he knew there was no way Lily Stone would remain simply a decorator in his life. She was going to play a part in his personal life, too. His skin tightened and his groin hardened in a rush. He didn't question his success because seduction had always been something he excelled at.

Her eyes widened as they met his, and he knew he'd lost ground on the seduction front because right now he felt elemental and knew that shone on his face. He wanted her with the gut-deep longing that was shockingly new to him. He knew about lust and desire but never had he felt it this intensely.

"Isn't it almost time for your meeting?" she asked, her voice husky with arousal.

He wondered what she'd do if he leaned down and kissed her. Thrust his tongue deep in her mouth the way he wanted to enter her body. It was a ridiculous reaction from a man so coldly controlled and smoothly sophisticated, yet she'd started a chain reaction in him.

"Yes," he said, grasping her arm above the elbow to escort her downstairs. Her flesh was soft under his hand, and she smelled like fresh-cut flowers with the dew still on them.

He walked Lily to her truck even though he knew he'd be late to his meeting. She hadn't said a word since they'd left the mansion.

She looked up at him as she opened the door to her vehicle. Desire danced in her eyes, and she leaned a little closer to him. Double or nothing, he thought.

"Will you have dinner with me tomorrow night?" he asked.

"Why?"

"I want to get to know you better."

"How much better?"

"On this date or in general?"

"In general," she said.

"Then, I want to know you as intimately as a man can know a woman."

"And afterward?"

"What afterward?"

"When you've gleaned all of my intimate secrets, then what?"

"Then life will point us in another direction."

"Separate ones?"

"Yes."

"I see."

"Lily, I'm not a settling-down kind of guy."

"I know."

"That doesn't mean you and I can't enjoy this attraction."

She didn't say anything.

"Why worry about the future? Let's take this one moment at a time. I'm only asking you to eat with me." Even though he knew he was planning to do more than eat. He was planning to seduce this sassy woman into his bed so that he could experience her fire and verve with every part of his body.

"One moment at a time," she said.

"Exactly."

"Okay, dinner, but at my place. Dress casually."

Preston nodded and waited until she climbed inside the cab of the old truck. She looked out of place in her vehicle, but it had been lovingly restored. It made him realize that she was the kind of woman who cherished the past. He'd been running from it all of his life.

She rolled down the window and handed him a business card. "My home address is on the back, come by around seven."

Preston watched her drive away and didn't like the feeling. His mind raced ahead as he plotted a way to have her without giving up himself.

When Lily had called Preston to say she couldn't keep their dinner plans, Preston's first instinct was to spend the night working as he usually did. But he finished early on the job site. He was one of those workaholic hands-on bosses. Jay had told him he worked too hard and to enjoy some of the sin in the Crescent City. Though she'd done nothing to encourage it, the image of Lily appeared in his head.

He had his secretary call Christian's Restaurant on Iberville and had swung by to pick up dinner. He told himself it was just good business to stop and see how the work was progressing on his resort, but he wanted to see Lily again. Wanted to prove to himself that she wasn't as sassy and sexy as he remembered. Wanted to prove to himself that she was nothing more than a subcontractor.

He pulled into the parking lot behind Sentimental Journey. Her shop had Old World elegance and New Orleans charm. Priceless antiques sat next to Mardi Gras masks and beads. It reminded him a little of the lady who owned and operated the place.

He sat in his eighty-five-thousand-dollar car listening to Mozart and doubting his actions. He'd always steered a true course to his destination, and this was an unplanned side trip. One that made no sense to the bottom line.

He thought about leaving, but that felt cowardly to him. He was a man's man. A man of action. Not someone who turned tail and ran. He could handle this situation and this woman.

He exited his Jaguar and pocketed the keys. The spicy Cajun food smelled aromatic. He figured she'd let him in for the food, if for nothing else.

He knocked on the screen door at the back. Harry Connick, Jr., played softly in the background. Lily glanced up and froze. He'd caught her off guard. Something he would wager not many people did.

"I brought dinner." Great. He sounded like some lame guy from a computer-dating service.

"I…uh…thanks."

"Can I come in?"

"Sure. Let me finish with this varnish, and I'll get the door."

He watched her through the mesh screen, feeling the way he had as a boy when he'd scored an unexpected soccer goal against an especially fierce rival team. The only thing he could imagine that would equal the sensation would be to kiss her. To feel her energy and passion up close and personal.

Three

––––––

"**T**hanks for bringing dinner," Lily said, as she opened the door for him.

"No trouble."

Her workroom was cluttered with antiques, most of them in a sad state of disrepair. "There's a table upstairs where Mae and I usually eat lunch."

"Lead on."

Lily was aware of how faded and worn her jean overalls were as she preceded Preston up the stairs. Though she knew it was probably only her imagination, she felt his gaze on her backside as she climbed the stairs.

The attic was large and spacious, sometimes serving as a guest room for her family when they all visited for Mardi Gras. There was an old butcher-block table that Lily had found at an estate sale three years ago and some ladder-back chairs she'd bought from a wholesaler last winter.

The kitchenette had a small refrigerator and microwave, and there was a tester bed pushed against one wall, covered with the first quilt Lily had ever made. Two wide windows let in the early-evening sunlight, and a big paddle fan kept the hot air circulating.

"Sorry there's no air-conditioning up here."

Preston removed his suit jacket and tie and rolled up his sleeves. There was a sprinkling of dark hair on his arms and at his neck. Lily wanted to touch it and see if it was as springy as it looked.

She took the dinner bags from Preston and began to set the table with mismatched plates. Preston took a bottle of French wine from one of the bags.

"Do you have a corkscrew?"

"In that basket by the microwave."

"I picked this up last summer at the vineyard in France," he said.

"I've always wanted to do one of those wine-tasting tours in Napa Valley."

"You should. Napa is beautiful."

"Maybe someday."

Lily and Preston took their seats, and the mournful sound of a saxophone from the street drifted through the open windows. Lily closed her eyes, enjoying the music and the scent of the food Preston had brought.

"I really needed a break. Thanks for doing this."

''I didn't mind. I'd been looking forward to seeing you again.''

''Too bad you didn't meet me sooner. Then I wouldn't have been postponed on your calendar twice.''

He smiled ruefully. ''I am a busy man.''

''When it suits you to be,'' she said.

''True.''

Preston wasn't the type of man to bring a pizza and beer, Lily thought as she bit into the shrimp Marigny he'd brought from one of the city's most expensive restaurants. The food was delicious, and Lily waited until Preston was halfway through his meal before bringing up the challenge he'd issued her the night before.

''I think I found a couple who married only for love.''

''Really?''

''My friend Kelly. I believe you mentioned you know her husband, Brit.''

''What makes you believe they married for love?''

''Kelly wouldn't marry a man she didn't love.''

''Brit would marry a woman he didn't love.''

''You're kidding.''

''No. He married her to arrange financing for the mansion. Her family has the connections he needed.''

Lily knew what he'd said was true. Kelly was the daughter of one of the wealthiest men in America, but she was also a dreamer. She and Kelly had spent many a night talking about the white knights that would ride up and rescue them.

"But they love each other now."

"Who's to say what's in another man's heart. He does seem to care deeply for her."

"I know it's more than caring."

"How do you know that, Lily?"

"Because he has a picture of her on his desk."

"That proves nothing. I know adulterous men who keep their wives' pictures on their desks."

"There was something in his eyes and in his voice when Kelly was in a room with us."

"Passion."

"Love," she countered.

"I'm not convinced," he said, abruptly.

"I guess I'll keep looking."

"Futilely."

"I'm going to prove you wrong."

The rest of the meal passed in silence. She cleaned the plates while Preston poured the last of the wine into their glasses and sat down on the sofa in front of the window. Lily put on an old Dizzy Gillespie record and joined him to watch the sun set over the city. The night sounds accompanied the sounds of the jazz trumpet.

"How did you end up raising your brothers?"

"My parents died when I was eighteen. My grandmother couldn't handle the boys, so that left me," Lily said. It still hurt to think of her parents gone. She missed them more than she'd ever imagined she could.

"How old were the boys?" he asked.

Lily settled back against the cushions of the old sofa and slid toward Preston. His body heat engulfed her. Knowing she was too close for comfort, she started to move away. She placed her hand on Preston's thigh to scoot forward.

His sharp intake of breath made her look up at him. He watched her with narrowed eyes. Lily longed to be the kind of woman who would say something witty, but she wasn't.

Her pulse beat furiously from her closeness to Preston. Maybe it was the wine. She rarely drank. She only knew her skin felt too tight, and the heat of the evening seemed cool against her skin.

"Sorry," she said. Where had this achy feeling come from?

"No problem, angel," he said, picking up her hand, brushing his lips against the back of it.

Shivers rushed through her, making her squirm. Her blood seemed to run heavier, pooling at the center of her body. Her nipples tightened under her T-shirt and denim overalls.

What had he asked her? Something about the boys ages?

"Beau was fifteen and Dash thirteen."

She had to keep her impulses under control, because she wanted to give into the forbidden sensuality his eyes promised, but couldn't. Preston Dexter wasn't a man who'd settle down. More than anything in the world, Lily wanted a husband to share her life and to give her babies.

She stood and paced to the window, unable to sit by Preston any longer. She wanted to give in to her wild impulses and fling her leg over his lap, straddle his hips and pull his mouth to hers for a deep kiss. But he wasn't the man for her, and her soul warned that heartache would follow.

"What are you afraid of, Lily?"

She glanced at the dark man sitting on her sofa. The man who'd experienced more of life than she even knew existed. A world outside of her beloved antiques and the past that she liked to bring to life.

"You."

"Not me. I represent nothing for you to fear."

She could have hedged. Her gut instinct urged her to, but the raw need in his eyes compelled her to speak honestly. "You make me want to be bold and daring when I never have been."

He smiled slightly, just the tiny curve of his firm mouth. She watched him closely, wishing she were a different kind of woman. The kind who'd really be able to handle the sophistication of Preston.

"Then isn't it time you started living?"

She knew what he wanted her to say, what her body wanted her to say, but her mind wanted self-preservation. "I need more than a summer fling."

He stood and walked to her—a man out of place in this environment but sure of himself in the world. "So do I."

He slid his hands into her hair and tilted her face toward his. The soft exhalation of his breath brushed across her mouth. Her lips tingled. She wanted to taste him and see if that strong sensual mouth would live up to her fantasies.

"Isn't it time you started living life for yourself, Lily?" he asked, and slowly lowered his head.

Unable to believe he had her in his arms, Preston barely brushed his lips against her eyelids and her cheeks. She was sweet and tempting, making a mockery of the control he'd always exercised over his libido.

Gently, because she seemed innocent, he traced her full lower lip, as he'd wanted to since he'd seen her nibble on it nervously in his office. She tasted of the expensive French wine they'd drunk with their meal, bold and rich, but also of the spicy Cajun spices, promising an embrace that would exceed his fantasies.

"Are you going to kiss me?" she asked, breathless. Her breasts brushed his chest lightly with each breath she took. He wanted to crush her to him. To feel the feminine mounds pressed against his chest. To rip away the layers of cloth that separated them and be together the way nature intended for man and woman to be.

"Do you want me to?" he countered. Tracing his tongue around her bow-shaped mouth. He loved the fact that she'd worried her lipstick off again. He was able to taste the very essence of Lily instead of some manufacturer's illusion of what a woman should be.

"Yes," she said on a sigh, her hands closing gently around his shoulders and pulling him closer.

He waited to see if she'd attack his mouth the way most of his dates did, but she didn't. She hesitated, her eyes half-closed and her breath held. He felt the tension vibrate through her.

He bent to her ear and brushed the softest kiss he could right below her lobe. She smelled faintly of flowers and the earthy scent of woman. There was something real about Lily, almost too real. He realized he didn't want her to watch him kiss her.

"Close your eyes," he said.

"Okay." She closed them. He let his gaze trace over her features. They were soft and ladylike. She was so feminine she made him feel like a big brute. The lessons he'd learned from faceless women in the past deserted him, and he could only react with instinct. He had to have her. Had to assert his will over her even if just in this small way.

He took her lower lip between his teeth and suckled there for a moment. The need to know all of her was a dangerous fire in his blood. The plump flesh tasted sweeter than he'd expected. She moaned, and her hands moved restlessly from his shoulders down his back.

He thrust his tongue into her mouth just the tiniest bit, teasing her with the flavor of him. She returned the foray with a tentative thrust of her own. His appetite whetted, he took her mouth deeply, her opened lips inviting him to do so. She held him tight as if afraid of where the embrace was leading.

Preston gave up thinking and reacted. His body ached to feel her softness beneath his. His mind supplied images of what she'd look like naked on that damned tester bed with the twilight spilling in through the windows and the seductive sounds of the saxophone and jazz trumpet filling the air.

She was every temptation he'd ever known. He wanted to act on those desires, but there was also something very sweet and trusting in the way she held him. As if she wasn't sure where things would lead next and he knew that she wasn't very experienced.

He'd suspected it yesterday when she'd kept tugging at her skirt, trying to conceal those long sexy legs. One of which was sliding between his own. He slid his hands down her back, cupping her behind in his hands. Her cheeks were firm and generous as he sank his fingers into her and pulled her closer to his aching flesh.

She rubbed against him without any true rhythm, just the demands of desire coursing through her veins. He had to stop now or her innocence wouldn't matter. They'd be twisting on that old mattress in the deepening night as his instincts urged.

He pulled back, brushing her wet, full lips with a lingering kiss and cradling her close to his aching body. He held her until his pulse stopped racing and his blood no longer rushed in his ears.

"That was one hell of a kiss, Lily."

She twisted in his arms, looking up at him with deep blue eyes that asked for honesty. "Why did you stop?"

"It was either stop now, or stop later on the bed after I'd buried myself deep within you."

"Oh."

"Don't worry, sweet Lily, you're safe with me."

"What if I don't want to be?"

"Don't tempt me, angel, because I'm hanging on to my control by a thread."

"I'm sorry. You're right. I said I didn't want a summer fling."

"You deserve more than that from me, and I don't know if I have it to give."

"How about if I prove that love exists in *your* life instead of in someone else's."

"Do you think you can?"

"I know I can."

"And if you don't."

"Then we'll both have had something rare and beautiful that we wouldn't have experienced otherwise."

"What is that?"

"Each other."

"You think I'm special?" he asked. No one ever had. He'd always been one of many spoiled rich prepschool boys who'd been given too much too soon.

She smiled and her eyes lit like a child being given a treat. "Yes, I do."

He thought she was special, too, but wouldn't tell her. Lily was the kind of girl who cared too deeply, and he was beginning to realize that if she couldn't teach him to love, then he'd teach her to doubt in love.

He didn't want to destroy the part of her that still believed in fairy tales.

Lily knew after that soul-shattering kiss that she'd taken a hell of a gamble, but she couldn't help herself. She felt as if Preston had reached past the barriers she'd used to protect herself all these years. For once she was totally in the present instead of reliving the past as she repaired a walnut, gateleg, William and Mary table. She knew she should focus on her work but all she could remember was his kiss.

He'd seduced her mouth slowly, taking control of her senses and making her willpower seem like a distant dream instead of something she'd clung to while raising her brothers. She'd never been intimate with a man. Never desired to do so, because most of the men she'd dated didn't want the responsibility of raising two boys even if they were almost grown.

Lily had been testing the boundaries of her newfound freedom. She'd dated two men since Beau had left for school last fall, but had found that she wasn't a woman for casual relationships. All these years she'd thought it was the boys keeping her from committing herself to a man, but she'd soon realized it was her own dreams.

All her life she'd been the mother hen. Taking care of those who needed caring, and she'd never met a man with more need than Preston Dexter. He'd stayed in her shop to keep her company and help her finish her work on a wrought-iron bedstead that would soon be gracing a lovely Creole cottage just off Bourbon Street.

She'd found the piece in a salvage yard outside the city earlier in the week, and the new owners of the cottage had paid double her fee for a rush delivery. Greedily she'd agreed to do the work, but now she was questioning whether it was worth it.

Nearly 10 p.m. and she was still dusty and dirty. It beat returning to her lonely, silent apartment. She hadn't realized how isolated she'd become from her friends in the years she'd been raising Dash and Beau. They'd all either moved on or married and now she spent most evenings at home reading or working late in her shop. On the plus side, Preston was still here with her, proving to her that he wanted more than her body.

Part of her wondered if that was his seduction plan. Was she flattering herself to think he had a plan relating to her? Did he want to lull her into believing that he cared for her before taking what he desired and leaving her behind? She shook her head. Obviously she was more tired than she'd thought. She wasn't cynical and she wasn't planning to be used. She wasn't Mona Stone's daughter for nothing. And if there was one area in her life where her mom had control it was over her men.

She glanced up and found Preston staring at her. She knew that she'd been looking at him with all the longing of a child looking through a candy shop window. She cleared her throat and spoke before he could.

"Look at this piece. Can't you just imagine the things it's seen."

Though he'd stayed, he seemed cold and arrogant. Much the same as the distant English noblemen in the gothic novels she loved to read. Would his home be dark and forbidding? It would match his looks and attitude.

"Oh, yes, angel," he said with a distinctive drawl.

Sex again. Growing up in the city that seemed to reek of sin, and not just once a year at Mardi Gras, should have inured her to the things he suggested with his silky tone and bedroom eyes, but it didn't. She'd always been a good Catholic girl.

"Not *those* things."

"What then?" he asked. Preston was polishing a brass wind-chime chandelier that she had to ship to a mansion in Atlanta on Monday.

"You know the life it's seen. Maybe a baby was born between these head- and footboards."

The only time she had a glimpse of his real personality was when he flirted with her. And she was so helplessly inept at it that he made her feel awkward. He winked at her. "I'm sure at least one was conceived."

His words made her hot. She'd been imagining them in that tester bed upstairs: his hard lean body over hers; the sounds of New Orleans pouring through the window with the scents of the Mississippi and the Gulf in the air; the warm breeze caressing their skin as they bonded together.

But she wanted more than sex from any man in her life. She'd never made love to a man, because she believed that love existed and Mr. Right was waiting out there for her. Preston made her doubt herself, and she didn't like that.

"Is sex all you think about?" she asked. Because when he was around it was all she thought about. She forgot about her dreams of getting married, wearing white and having a couple of babies with a nice guy who'd be content to buy a Creole cottage with a white picket fence and raise kids in her hometown.

"Lately it is."

With Preston working beside her on the steamy August night it was easy to believe the desire coursing through her body was something other than just lust. Since it was the one thing he understood, she answered honestly. "Me, too."

"Dammit, Lily, it wouldn't hurt you to lie once in a while."

She looked away. She'd never guarded her words. She'd always spoken straight from the gut and more often than not it had brought more trouble than a ship full of pirates intent on pillaging.

Tucking her polishing cloth into the back pocket of her overalls, she stood. She didn't trust herself around this man. He called to the dangerous part of her that had always longed for adventure but had never been brave enough to set foot outside of Orleans Parish. "Let's call it a night."

He crossed to her and stopped so close she could

count the individual eyelashes surrounding his gray eyes. "I didn't mean that the way it sounded. Your words go straight through me."

For the first time she understood there was more to Preston than he wanted the world to see. She'd suspected it when he'd hatched the love dare, but his words just now confirmed it. Could she break through the barriers he used to protect himself without getting hurt? Did she want to?

He stood so closely that if she leaned forward the tiniest bit, she'd brush his body. She teetered toward him before she realized what she'd done and retreated a half step. "I don't understand this attraction to you, Preston."

He said nothing. She knew he was a man accustomed to dating and bedding women. She'd seen his picture in the society pages since he'd moved to New Orleans in the early summer, but she wasn't used to this type of man. It's just business, she told herself. "I know we'd both be better off apart."

"I don't think I would be," he said.

"Why not?"

"I've been alone too long."

"Me, too," she said softly.

He brushed a butterfly-soft kiss against her forehead. "Don't let me hurt you."

I won't, she thought. But inside she didn't know if she'd be able to protect herself from him. There were emotions he brought seething to the surface of her soul that she'd never grappled with before and honestly didn't know how to control.

Four

Two days later Lily still wasn't sure what to do about Preston and the attraction she felt for him. She'd invited Preston to accompany her to an antique importer just outside of town. It was a steamy New Orleans day, typical of late summer, and she knew riding in her '59 Chevy truck without air-conditioning would be hot and uncomfortable.

Even though it was ten minutes before they were scheduled to leave, when he was interested in meeting with someone, Preston was always very punctual. And as he slid out of the car, she acknowledged he was always very attractive.

She'd pored over books and the Internet trying to find romantic couples to use to convince him love existed. She didn't know which of them would hold out longer. Her or Preston. He had a secret ally in her traitorous body. She'd woken up in a sweat last night, dreaming of him moving over her in the bed. How was she going to prove love when she was obsessed with sex?

She had her doubts. Love was hard work and in the end she knew that it required effort and belief on the part of both partners in a relationship. Some things were worth the risk, she thought, but her hands continued to sweat and her body tingled.

Preston wasn't a man who'd learn to love easily, but she'd decided she wasn't going to let him fly out of her life as easily as he'd drifted into it. Actually, she thought it hadn't been all that easy. She scooted closer to the workroom window so that she could watch Preston. He stopped to talk to Leroy, her deliveryman.

The deep sounds of his voice drifted with the warm breeze through the open window. Lily closed her eyes and let both wash over her. There was something about a man with a deep voice—

"Va-va-voom!" Mae said from behind her.

"Mae," Lily chided, hoping none of her lustful thoughts were revealed on her face.

"Is he yours?" she asked. Mae wasn't in the market for a man, having married her high school sweetheart last year.

No, she thought, but I want him to be. "Maybe."

"Be careful, Lily. He's the World Series, and you've been having trouble in the minors."

Lily chuckled. "You don't even know what that means. Why do you try to use sports analogies?"

"You know what I mean. I've dated that kind, and they are only good for one thing."

"Sex?" she asked without thinking.

Mae arched her a look that told Lily she'd revealed more than she'd intended to. "No, Lily, heartache."

"Advice received."

"But not accepted."

"Not yet."

"Just be careful, honey."

Mae left quietly. Lily continued to watch through the window. Maybe Mae was right. He was out of her league. She knew, heck, he knew it, too. But she wanted to know the Preston who'd told her he was tired of being lonely. Because that man wasn't rich as Midas and needed something that plain Lily Stone could give him.

He stepped into her cluttered workroom as if he owned the place. Moving with confidence through dirty, broken pieces of the past. She'd told him to dress casually, but he looked ready to step onto a yacht. Didn't the man own a pair of jeans? And did he always have to look so arrogant.

"Hello, angel."

His gaze lingered on her mouth but he kept five inches of space between them. Fire swept through her body and the tingle in her skin increased. She wanted to clutch at his shoulders and pull him closer to her for a welcoming kiss, to feel his tongue sweep deep inside leaving no part of her untouched and making her long for another taste of him. But their relationship wasn't at that comfortable level yet. He wasn't her man. No matter how much she wanted him to be.

Though he was strong and sure of himself, he wooed her carefully because he wanted her and knew she was unsure. Her nipples tightened, and she leaned closer to him, brushing against his chest.

He groaned deep in his throat. "Want to play?"

More than she wanted her next breath, but she wasn't sure she was ready to pay the piper at the end of this dance. She stepped back. No matter what her body said, her mind wasn't ready to give in to Preston. "Not today."

"Angel, you're killing me," he said, but winked at her.

"You're in a good mood."

He nodded, absently picking up a sterling goblet and twirling it in one hand. "I just signed a deal for some property in Barbados."

"Congratulations," she said, and meant it. But part of her realized he'd be leaving some day. Even if she could convince him forever existed, he wasn't planning to stay.

"Come on, if we're not there when they open at eleven, all the good stuff will be gone."

"Then by all means, let's hurry." He smacked her on the derriere as he walked past her.

"Pres, I don't trust you in this mood."

"Neither do I," he said.

"That's not very reassuring."

"I know. Still going to prove to me love exists?"

"Yes. As a matter-of-fact, I'm planning a lovers-through-time thing to show you the different ways that love has been expressed."

"What a treat."

"You do sarcasm well."

"It's a gift."

"I hope you lose it."

They bantered back and forth until they reached her truck. She waited for him to get in the cab. As he climbed into her painfully neat but worn vehicle, she tried to ignore that he didn't fit in her world, but the image stuck in her mind as she drove away.

Preston let the warm Louisiana breezes waft over him through the open window. The hot setting sun lulled him into a feeling of almost contentment. He'd spent the day in an import yard going through dirty antiques and loading them in the back of Lily's pickup.

Though the work had been hard, he'd found it fulfilling in a way he'd never imagined blue-collar work to be. He'd really enjoyed himself and made a mental note to find some way of thanking Lily for giving him this experience.

Lily concentrated on her driving, and he had to admit she wasn't extremely skilled. She kept to the right hand lane and drove with care, but frequently looked at him, making eye contact as she drove. Swerving toward the center and back again. The bed of her pickup was piled high with furniture and covered with a tarp. He'd offered to drive for her but had received a quelling glance in return.

No one ever dared to stand up to him, but she did. It was as if she didn't care about his position or power. And maybe she didn't.

There was something very real about Lily and at the same time something ethereal. She moved with quick decisive actions, but when she touched her beloved antiques there was languidness to her movements, as if she really touched the past.

That bothered him because he'd been running from the past for most of his life and she seemed to wallow in it. To surround herself with bits and pieces of it instead of focusing on the future.

A rush of adrenaline pumped through his body. A big part of it was desire for Lily and her luscious body, but another part was the thrill of riding in the car with her. The wind in his hair and the sound of Dixieland jazz in the air.

Lily was dressed in faded denim jeans that should have been illegal. They'd been washed too many times and clung to her legs and backside like a lover. She'd discarded a man's work shirt earlier, leaving her clad only in a tight little T-shirt that accentuated the firm mounds of her breasts. All he'd been able to concentrate on while she'd been looking over antiques was whether her nipples would be brown or pink.

Would they respond to his mouth the way they had

to the cool air-conditioning in the manager's office at the import yard? Would she let him suckle her?

"Did you really have a Louis XIV settee in your childhood home?"

Preston shifted on the seat to relieve the tension in his crotch. "Yes. My nanny and I used to sit on it to read bedtime stories."

"You had a nanny?" she asked.

"Yes. She raised me until I was eight."

"What was she like?"

Preston thought about it. Greta Parcell had been all that was warm and kind. Loving in a way his mother never had been. In fact, he'd thought Greta was his mother until she left abruptly. "She was a paid servant, Lily. What do you think she was like?"

"I'm sure she was very motherly."

"She was."

"My grandmother used to employ Dora to help around the house, and she's practically part of the family now. Do you still keep in touch with your nanny?"

"No, she took another position when I was eight and I've never heard from her again." Preston still remembered how he begged her to stay. But in the end his father had been right. Money was a powerful motivator, more powerful than any of the emotions despite what people might say they'd do anything for money.

"Did your mother take over raising you then?"

Preston glanced out the window at Lake Pontchartrain. Leisure boaters and fishermen vied for space on the water. He didn't want to dwell on his mother. He wondered if he could coax Lily onto his yacht tonight. Take her out under the stars, let the rocking of the boat seduce her as he wooed her carefully into his arms.

"No," he said quietly.

He put his fingers over Lily's lips before she could ask another question. He didn't want to talk about his family any more or answer any of her questions. He wanted to steer her back onto safer ground. "How are you going to prove that true love exists in my life?"

"By showing you the love that is already there."

"You're going to have to dig deep to find any in my life."

"I don't think so," she said, quietly. She stared at him for a minute until a honking horn drew her attention back to the road. Waving apologetically out the window while Preston observed her in silence.

He wanted Lily like he'd wanted no other woman. But he didn't want to hurt that rose-colored view of the world she had. She was a shrewd businesswoman, he'd seen the evidence with his own eyes as she'd bargained at the import yard but a part of her had remained innocent about life.

"I thought you mentioned lovers in history."

"I did. My theory here is that love is kind of sneaky. Are you ready?"

"As ever."

"Do you know the tale of Tristan and Isolde? It's a Celtic tale from the twelfth century."

"I'm not familiar with it. But then, I've never really been interested in the past," he said.

"Well, it's a good thing I am. You're going to love this tale of passion and devotion that withstands all trials."

"I can't wait."

Preston rested his head against the backrest and watched Lily drive and talk. Sometimes swerving into the other lane as she became more involved in her story. Her large sunglasses covered her eyes but when she came to the ending where they both died and two trees with their branches entwined sprung up from their graves, tears spilled down her face.

"How's that for true love?"

He realized then what a fragile flower Lily was. She wasn't the tough gal who negotiated with the butcher-faced man at the import yard. She was a closet romantic who probably waited for her fairy-tale prince to come and sweep her away to his castle.

But Preston had never been too good at happily-ever-after. Not once had anything lasted long enough for him to look beyond the surface of what his money had purchased.

"Preston?"

"Great tale. But it's not real life."

"I know. I'm priming the pump and getting you thinking about epic love. You'll find it yourself in life once you learn what to look for."

"You're sure of that?"

"No, but I'm hoping."

He was hoping, too, because he liked the spark that

Lily brought to his life and he wanted to keep it for a while longer. He liked the challenge she represented.

Lily hated social situations that required her to know which fork to use. She knew them, but her nerves usually guaranteed she'd drop something before the night was over. Though Preston had said that a night in his home wasn't cause for nerves, she was agitated just the same.

He'd been watching her the way a lion watches its prey. Gauging her reactions to him and carefully keeping his distance all day at the import yard so his invitation to dinner had caught her off guard. She'd almost said no. But he'd leaned closer, the scent of his cologne surrounded her and she'd been unable to say no.

Her only alternative was a lonely night at home watching public television. So now she stood in the foyer of his condo and wished she'd chosen television. Soft music played in the background, and candles provided the only light.

"Let me take your bag," Preston said, leading her into the living room. A bank of windows looked down on the French Quarter. The evening stars were bright, and she knew from experience that the night air would be filled with chattering tourists, hawkers and jazz music. But tonight she and Preston were ensconced in air-conditioned splendor.

She rubbed her bare arms and looked idly around the room. It was decorated with cutting-edge furniture all chrome and glass. Sleek leather sofas and plush velvet pillows. An avant-garde painting hung on one wall and a bank of mirrors lined another. Lily thought she looked out of place in the room.

She glanced quickly away. She'd always imagined how the rich and famous lived but this didn't seem too great to her. The plush carpeting invited her to kick off her shoes and run her toes through the pile, but she knew Preston would never do such a thing.

"Wine?"

She nodded. Preston's shirt was open at the collar and she glimpsed the hair curling at his neck. She trembled as she reached for the wineglass.

He motioned for her to be seated on one of the leather sofas. Miles Davis's "Summer Night" played in the background. The warm, smooth trumpet melody highlighted the loneliness of the room and the man who lived there.

Lily perched on the edge of the seat afraid to move, lest she spill her merlot. For the first time since she'd met him she had nothing to say. She acknowledged she was out of her depth with him and realized that put her at a disadvantage.

Though he sat next to her, they were separated like the French and Spanish inhabitants of early New Orleans. A respectable five inches separated them, but the heat of his body reached her in waves. He smelled of expensive cologne and a scent that was uniquely Preston. She leaned closer to him before she realized what she was doing.

Like a debutante in search of the elusive gold bean

in a King Cake, she wanted him. The King Cake was baked only during Mardi Gras and whoever got the bean received their wish. For once she wanted to be like the city she'd grown up in: the city had been built of saints and sinners, but she was tired of being the good girl.

The revelation startled her, and Lily deliberately scooted away from Preston. Trying for a hint of normalcy, she said, "Your place is very nice."

"It mirrors my penthouse in Manhattan. I like to feel at home wherever I go."

She had a glimpse of the man behind the corporate success and generations of wealth. It revealed to her the craving she doubted he was even aware of—the craving for home. Suddenly she knew she wasn't going to just have to prove to him love existed, she was going to have to show him that family and friends were the key to nurturing love.

"Why did you ask me here tonight?" she asked before taking a sip of her wine. She knew that he was uncomfortable with her attempts to show him love in the world. But she was determined that Preston would learn to love.

"So that I could seduce you," he said in a deep voice.

She sputtered, choking on her wine. His words sent tiny contractions throughout her body. Tightening her breasts against the lacy cups of her bra and making her feminine place moist. If only seduction were that simple, she thought, but the consequences would have long-reaching effects.

"Relax, little red, I'm not the big bad wolf ready to pounce." He took her goblet from her and set it on the beveled-glass coffee table.

"This place makes me uncomfortable," she said. His gray eyes watched her carefully, and she wondered if he felt that same nervous-tingly-anticipating emotion she did.

He settled his arm against the back of the couch, his hand resting innocently on her shoulder. "Really? I thought I did."

Lily's pulse picked up, and she barely understood what Preston was saying. Her breasts felt full as his finger moved idly back and forth on her bare upper arm. Prickles shot from her shoulder throughout her body.

"Angel, do I make you nervous?"

"Yes, but I'm getting used to you in my world. Just seeing you in your own is different." She had trouble holding on to the thread of the conversation. She wanted to slip closer to him on the sofa and feel his masculine body pressed against her softer one. She wanted to pull him closer for the kiss he hadn't claimed when she arrived. She wanted something she'd never wanted from a man before and that scared her.

"Don't start treating me with the respect my position usually commands. I won't know how to deal with you."

She smiled wryly. Here was the Preston she'd come

to know. She had a feeling he was just coming to know this side of himself, as well. There was a lot of himself that Preston walled off from the world. This Preston made her want to hold him closer and show him the world she'd come to know.

"Don't worry. I'm sure you can keep up."

"No doubt."

He still rubbed at her shoulder and if they didn't get up soon, she'd be moving closer to him. She scooted a few inches away from his touch.

"What's the matter, angel?" he asked, his eyes harder than diamonds. She shivered a little as she realized another facet of this amazing man.

Honesty had always been one of her credos even when it left her in an uncomfortable position. "I'm not ready to make love to you tonight, Preston. But I think you could make me believe I am."

He cursed under his breath and picked up his wineglass, draining it in one swallow. "I know that."

"Why did you really invite me here?" she asked for the second time.

He looked at her, and Lily thought it was to make sure she could handle the truth of his words. She tried to look brave and gave him a weak smile.

"Because I want you and you want me. It's time we really learned about each other."

"Why?" She couldn't for the life of her figure out why he'd want to know more about her, because the man who lived in this apartment was used to successful seduction.

''Because sooner or later I'm going to have you, and I don't want you to regret it.''

She thought about that for a minute. ''I'd never regret anything I did with you.''

He reached out to touch her cheek gently. ''I hope not, angel. I hope not.''

Five

Preston knew he'd almost lost Lily earlier in the living room, but here on the balcony, with the remains of a five-star dinner on the table between them, things were different. Maybe it was because the city she loved was spread beneath them. A thriving sea of humanity with all its glories and faults.

They'd talked about books they liked, and he wasn't surprised to learn Lily preferred fiction that had a happy ending. She was well versed in ancient mythology and had regaled him with love stories from classic Greece. He didn't believe that learning about the toils some lovers went through to stay together was going to change his mind about modern love, but he appreciated the time she was putting into the project.

"Do you really think love is worth all that?" he asked after she told the tale of Odysseus, which he'd heard before.

"You're missing the point, deliberately I think. Love is the reward you get after overcoming the tough times in life."

"Interesting. Have you been rewarded?" Preston knew he'd never been rewarded. He'd often taken pleasure in people and in possessions but he'd never known anything lasting from them. Even the car he drove would be replaced, probably next year.

"I wouldn't be here with you if I had. I do have the love of my brothers and grandmother, though."

"What of your parents?" he asked.

"You know that story. But they loved me when they were alive. Didn't yours?"

"No."

He knew she wanted to know more, but he wasn't going to bare all for her. He didn't talk about his family with anyone. Not even his closest acquaintances knew his true feelings about them. And he would never reveal them. He had been raised to be polite, to buy what he wanted and take what he could. Never look back, he remembered his father saying as they watched his mother leave them for what would be the final time to go to one of her many younger lovers.

"Do you want to talk about it?" she asked, her small hand resting lightly on his own.

He shook his head. "Not tonight."

"We're never going to get to know each other if we don't talk about what's made us who we are, Preston."

"Hard work and ambition have shaped me," he said, bluntly. He wanted her but didn't want her prying. He wanted to probe her depths, to find the secrets of her soul but at the same time he wanted to stay safe within his own world.

"Me, too," she said with a small smile.

"Tell me what it's like to own your small business."

"It's hard work. Grandmother wanted my parents to take over, but they were archeologists and traveled all over the world on digs. They always left us behind, and Grandmother said she wasn't losing another generation to the world, so she raised me to love the past and her shop."

"Do you like what you do?"

"I wouldn't do anything else."

He realized she meant that and longed to feel the same about something in his life. His job didn't give him the sense of satisfaction that was radiating from Lily.

"What about you?" she asked. "What's shaped you?"

"My dad had a sudden heart attack when I was in my last year of college. He died instantly."

Her fingers tightened on his and he was tempted to squeeze back but didn't. He wanted to find the safe neutral ground with her. Sex and the present but not the past, he warned himself.

"Anyway, Dexter Resorts was in some trouble. The

board of directors wanted to sell off the different properties. I convinced them to give me a year to turn things around.''

''And you did it,'' she said.

''Damn straight.''

''Because you didn't want to lose what your father had worked so hard for?''

His father had been a bit of a playboy, spending more money than the resort chain could ever have made. So following in his dad's footsteps had never been a goal. In fact, he'd never analyzed too closely just why he'd had to save Dexter Resorts.

''What do you do for fun?'' she asked, leaning across the table. He wondered if the wine had made her a little tipsy.

''Work. You?'' he asked, finishing off his own glass of merlot.

She batted her eyelashes at him and smiled like the temptress she was when she relaxed and dropped her guard. Heat shot straight to his groin, and he had a hard time concentrating on her words. ''I play a mean game of basketball.''

He eyed her frame. Soft and sexy, Lily was everything that was feminine and ladylike. Also she barely topped five-three in heels. ''Sure you do, angel.''

The temptress disappeared, and the hoyden who'd challenged him to believe in love reappeared. ''I could beat you anyday.''

This was the lady he knew would go up in flames

in his arms. The adventuresome woman who Lily tried to keep under wraps. "Prove it."

"Okay, let's go. We can play at my shop. I have a hoop in the alley." She stood up, hands on her hips. Challenging and ready for a fight.

Preston grabbed her hand and tugged her closer to his chair. Her sundress was made of some sort of flimsy material and the light from inside his apartment illuminated her body. She was so tempting. One tug and she'd be in his lap. "Not tonight. Tomorrow afternoon."

"Great. I look forward to it. I've always wanted to see a man eat crow." Her eyes sparkled, and suddenly resisting her wasn't something he could do.

"Really?" he asked, pulling her closer to him. She leaned down so that they were face-to-face. Her breath brushed over his mouth, and he closed his eyes so that he wouldn't be able to see the sweet innocence in hers.

"Yes," she said breathlessly.

Her chest rose and fell rapidly, and her nipples were beaded against the flimsy bodice of her dress. His hands shook with the need to touch her more intimately.

"Want to make it a little more interesting?" he asked, hanging on by a thread.

"With a wager?" she whispered. Her gaze on his mouth. He brushed his mouth gently over hers. Back and forth, teasing them with barely a glimpse of each other.

"Oh, yeah," he said.

"Name your price," she said, licking her lips.

You in my bed, he thought. But that was the surest way to drive her out of his apartment and his life. "An evening together, winner's choice."

Her free hand came up to cup his face, and for a moment he forgot about seduction. Forgot about spending the evening in that big king-size bed just a few feet away. Forgot that she wanted from him the one thing he'd always feared.

"I'll make you see that love does exist," she promised.

"I'll make love to you until you forget about girlish notions of love," he returned, turning his face in her palm and biting the flesh.

"Should we shake on it?"

"Hell, no," he said, pulling her down on his lap and taking the kiss he'd been dying to claim all evening.

Lily knew that she could beat Preston in a game of one-on-one. She'd been playing basketball everyday of her life. Her father had gone to school on a basketball scholarship, and whenever he'd come home he'd always taken her to the courts to play.

Dash had been All-State in high school, and Beau had played in college, and she could beat both of them when she concentrated on her game. But then, she didn't think of them as men. She'd never noticed anyone on the court apart from her game strategy, but she noticed Preston.

Actually it went beyond noticing. She told herself

that it was due to the fact that she'd never seen him in anything other than business clothing, but she didn't know if that was true. His athletic shorts and tank top were new, but fit him like a second skin. He moved across the court with grace and ease, and she knew she'd have to concentrate to beat him.

But she couldn't help notice the rippling of muscles as he made a free throw or the power in his legs as he dribbled down the court. He leaped in the air and made a throw that would have done a pro proud.

The now-familiar excitement started pumping through her veins. Dammit. This was the one time she really wanted to win, and he was distracting her with his body. She glared at him, wanting to believe he knew what he was doing to her but feared he didn't. He hadn't even kissed her when he'd arrived. A first since he'd told her he wanted her in his bed.

She had to get her mind on the game. There was more at stake here than she wanted to admit, but she knew she had to win. He passed the ball to her, and she practiced dribbling down the court and took her shot. It hit the backboard and bounced out of bounds.

"Nice try, angel," Preston said with a wink.

"Never let the competition see your strengths," she said. Damn, she never missed from the free-throw line. Breathe, she reminded herself, and don't think about his body.

"What are you showing me?"

"Nothing. I'm letting you build false confidence."

"Oh, yeah?"

"Yeah," she said, wishing it was true.

"Ready to start?" he asked.

"Whenever you are, pretty boy."

"Was that an insult?"

"Did you take it as one?"

He eyed her carefully and tossed her the basketball. "Ladies first."

They played fast and furious, as if the outcome were more important than they'd both been telling each other it was. Lily had never met a man who'd treated her as an equal on the court the way Preston did. She had to admit he was a better player than she'd given him credit for being, but he wasn't better than her.

Also, he wasn't above using any means at his disposal to win. When he blocked her as she went to score the winning point, his hand brushed her breast. The ball bounced out off the rim and Lily stood trembling, afraid to move.

"You missed," he said, his voice husky with exertion and sexual tension.

"That's cheating," she said, trying to ignore the ache in her nipples. At least she was wearing a sports bra. Maybe he wouldn't notice.

"Purely accidental," he said, but his gaze lingered on her chest. She had the impulse to cross her arms over her breasts but didn't give in to it. Instead she thrust her shoulders back, watching as he swallowed visibly and looked away.

Did she affect him as deeply as he did her? Lily decided to try a little experiment. She blocked him as he tried to take a shot and this time used all the tools in her feminine arsenal. This was man against woman, she realized.

Turning, she used the back of her body to block him and then as he coiled to jump she thrust her hips back toward him, brushing against his groin. She took a step forward; planning to excuse herself for the below-the-belt touch, but Preston was quicker than she'd expected.

Letting the ball roll off the court and grabbing her waist, he pulled her closer to him. His ragged breath brushed against her neck, making gooseflesh spread throughout her body.

"Is this how you want to play?" he asked, dropping small biting kisses along her neck.

Lily couldn't even think. It seemed she did have some effect on him and his control. She knew he wanted to keep her in the role of a woman he was seducing, but she wasn't going to let him. Because last night at his place she'd realized that Preston needed everything she had to give him. He needed more than her body and her company. He needed someone to show him how to love with his soul.

She wanted him but feared the wild impulses racing through her body. He made her react and damn the consequences. But she knew that the sinner always had to repent. Her instincts screamed for her to take what he was offering, to know what it was like to really be a woman. But her heart warned she'd get hurt. And she wasn't ready to risk her heart.

She was already energized from going toe-to-toe with him on the court. She wanted to win the game there, but she'd rather win on the personal level. She'd rather have him at her mercy here, man to woman than player to player.

She shifted back against him, enjoying the feel of his hard body behind her softer one. Enjoying the pressure of his body against her. Enjoying the fact that he could make her feel as if each of her senses was on overload.

Preston groaned, his hands coming up to cup her breasts. She felt like a tease, because she knew that she wasn't going to let him make love to her until she believed he could love her.

"Are you forfeiting?" She forced herself to ask.

A silence, broken only by their breathing, filled the air. The sounds of cars passing on the road and pedestrians on the street provided distant background music. The city pulsed around them and through them. And though they weren't visible to any of the passersby Lily suddenly felt embarrassed by what she'd done. By what she'd allowed to happen.

"I'm sorry," she said in a rush.

"Don't be."

"I'm not a tease," she said. Say it again, maybe you'll believe it.

"Lily, angel, I started this."

"No, you didn't. I'd been lusting after you since you showed up."

He smiled one of his sweet smiles that made her

know there was a wonderful lonely man inside of him waiting to get out. "That's good to know."

"I'm..."

"Overreacting," he said. He hugged her close, and the wild desire that was pulsing through her was oddly quieted by the strength in his arms.

"I think we'd better call this game a draw."

"Why?"

"Because I'm in no condition to finish."

She glanced down at the distended front of his shorts. It didn't give her a rush of power or a feeling of victory over him. It made her feel a little ashamed that she'd tried to cheat to win. She never had before.

"I think you would've won," she said, stepping back from him.

"Lily, there's no shame in what you did."

"I've been trying to tell you that lust without love is something you could find with anyone."

"I already know that."

"Than why did I just treat you like some boy toy?"

"Because love really is a myth, and attraction is a powerful impetus."

"I've always told myself that I was waiting for love, waiting for my Prince Charming to come along and awaken me but suddenly I'm alive and filled with desire and..."

"There's no Prince Charming," he said, and turned to walk away.

Lily watched him go, knowing she'd wounded him

but unsure how to fix it. Because in her heart she believed he could be her Prince Charming.

Preston stayed away from Lily and the White Willow House for two weeks. He'd flown to New York and partied with his socialite friends. But the lifestyle left him cold, and though Lily had hurt him with her words, he acknowledged they were the truth.

Now, standing in the refinished atrium of White Willow House, Preston realized he'd been running away because he felt like he'd come home. As though he'd found the one place he belonged and it wasn't his familiar environment.

Lily started when she saw him. Preston didn't fool himself that it was surprise coursing through her. He knew from the way she'd played basketball to win that it was anger controlling her now. He may have gained ground on convincing her love didn't exist, but he was pretty sure he'd lost leagues on the seduction front.

Part of him knew it was for the best. She was too good for him. He'd realized how fragile she could be that night in his home. He didn't want to be a big hulking masculine beast, tearing at the safe haven of her world, but he knew that he was.

She turned away as he approached and walked across the marble floor with a stride that would have done a marine proud.

"Lily."

She stopped but didn't turn around. The faded denim overalls she wore should have made her look out of place in the plush hotel lobby surrounded by her antiques. But she seemed more at home among the pieces she'd picked and refurbished than he felt.

He'd lost her. He felt it deep in his gut where he'd felt Greta's betrayal when he'd been eight and unsure of the world. It ticked him off because he was old enough to know better.

"It seems I've won our bet," he said silkily. Needing to reach through the barriers she'd erected around herself to keep him out.

She glanced over her shoulder, her blue eyes cold instead of warm and welcoming. Even that first afternoon in his office she'd at least had the gleam of challenge in her eyes—today nothing. She was still sexy as hell with her short hair mussed and clinging to her face and neck. He longed to taste her skin there. To linger as he hadn't trusted himself to on the basketball court.

"Which one?" she asked.

"The love one. It seems even you have decided it's not worth the risk. Good thing I'm not waiting at home for you in a house filled with infidels."

She pivoted on her heel and marched over toward him. Her chest rose and fell, and her lips narrowed. She should have looked like a prim schoolmarm, but no teacher had ever affected him the way Lily did. Straight to the groin with enough heat to power the electrical needs of New York for a month.

"How dare you?" she asked, jabbing him in the chest with her index finger.

"I dare anything I please," he said with all the arrogance he'd learned from his parents. But he didn't know how to handle this situation. He'd never been near anything that vaguely resembled this woman or her approach to life. She wasn't staying by his side because of his money. Why, then?

"You're the one who ran away," she said.

She always went for the jugular, and while he could admire her style, he admitted that it hurt. Especially since the innate vulnerability in her face always stopped him from reciprocating. He was sure someday someone was going to disillusion her, but he didn't want it to be him. "I was on a business trip."

"Is that what they're calling it these days?" she said. There was more than anger in her body, and as he searched her eyes, he thought he saw hurt, as well.

"What exactly are you implying, Lily?" he asked, because although he'd partied every night, he'd been in town for a business meeting that couldn't be rescheduled.

"I read the papers like everyone else, Preston. Did you think because we're in the South that your escapades wouldn't reach us? You're a big-time businessman, and New Orleans likes nothing better than debauchery."

Must have been a slow day for news if he'd made the papers. Usually only acquisitions and mergers brought him press coverage. "Hell, angel, this keeps getting better and better. You say debauchery like it's a disease."

"Isn't it?" she asked, most of the anger gone from her voice, leaving only that hurt he didn't want to see. How was he going to mend this?

He considered how much he needed to touch her. When they were together and touching, things were right between them. He didn't fool himself that a mere brush of his hand down her arm would right this perceived wrong, but he needed to do something to erase the damage in her eyes. "To some."

"To me?" she asked.

He took her hand in his. It was so much smaller than his was. He circled her palm with his forefinger. "Not to you. You have a soul for adventure."

"Then why do I prefer the home life?"

Preston wasn't sure he knew her well enough to answer, but from the beginning he'd felt she was hiding from something. "You're afraid of yourself."

She wrinkled her nose at him. "How did you turn this back to me? I'm not the one who was in the papers with a gorgeous blonde."

"Was I?" he asked, wishing he'd thought to find the photographer and pay the man to keep his film unexposed. But it was too late; the damage had been done.

"Don't play games with me. I believed you were serious when you said we wouldn't be better off apart. Did you have a change of heart?"

She wanted more than he felt comfortable giving, but he knew he would need to show her some of himself if he wanted her to stay. And suddenly he knew that he did. It was more than the desire hardening his body every time he looked at her. He wasn't sure what, but he needed to be with her. To enjoy her smiles and laughter. To seduce her into his bed and life so that he could bathe in her sunshine for at least a little while.

"I needed to get away, and this business trip had been scheduled. I'm within an inch of taking you, angel. It's not every day that I take the pure and noble route. Believe me I won't do it again."

"I thought you at least cared for me."

I do, he thought, but didn't say anything out loud. "Lily, fate tends to demand a price for that kind of deep emotion."

"I can't imagine going through life without caring."

"You should try it."

"Why?"

"It's pain free."

She closed the gap between them. Cupping his cheek in her palm. She brushed her thumb across his bottom lip. "Oh, Preston."

He didn't say anything else to her, because he knew he'd come close to losing her and he didn't want to lose her yet. He didn't want to admit that she mattered to him in the least, but he knew he'd miss her smile if he never saw it again.

Six

The loud Zydeco music swirled around them like the sounds of Mardi Gras, fun, frivolous but masking something deeper. It was the lyrics that were anything but light and funny. The bride, her cousin Marti, and her new husband, Brad, danced with all the fervor that they felt. There was an exciting sort of sexual tension in the air as bodies brushed together and swung apart.

"Champagne?" Preston asked.

She nodded and accepted the flute from him. It was really sparkling wine, but she doubted any of her family or friends realized. She knew that Preston would. He was easily the best-dressed man there, but he was relaxed and charming, making her realize how easily he flitted through the throngs of people without them realizing they were only seeing a mirage—not the real man.

"How did you like the ceremony?" she asked trying to think of anything but how good he looked dressed in black and white.

"A little long but very nice."

The high Catholic Mass had lasted for an hour, and Lily had been aware of others shifting in their seats around them, but Preston had been focused on the ceremony. She'd always loved the rituals of her church and had been glad to see that Preston appreciated them, too.

"Brad and Marti married for love," Lily said, sipping her drink.

"They do seem to be infected with the love bug," he said dryly.

"Ha! So you admit it exists." She felt giddy. Probably from being around those closest to her. Probably from the champagne. Probably from sitting so close to Preston, having his cologne tempt her senses and his wit tempt her mind.

"Hell, angel, I admit that many people believe love exists. That doesn't mean it's real." He scooted his chair closer to her, draping his arm over her shoulders. The weight was pleasant on the back of her neck. His fingers kept beat to the music against her shoulder. It was a light brush of his finger against her skin and made warmth spread throughout her body, pooling at her center. She shifted in the chair and hoped he wouldn't notice.

But those clear gray eyes missed nothing. He raised one eyebrow and bent to kiss her below her ear. She shivered and shifted again. She wanted to pull him to her and kiss him as she had that night in his apartment. She wanted to feel his strong hard body against hers.

He distracted her and made her forget she wanted something from him that he doubted he could ever feel. "How can I prove that to you?"

He glanced away from her. His touch stopped, and she felt him pull into himself, searching for an answer. She knew that what she'd done when she'd blindly challenged him would open them to a world of pain if she failed. She was asking a man who'd forgotten how to hope to try again. If she failed, Lily realized, they'd both be affected. She'd been worrying about herself. Trying to figure out how she'd protect herself from needing him too much, but Preston had been opening up to her. Letting her see the things he needed.

"How do you make love stay?" he asked. She knew he really wanted to know.

She didn't have an answer for him, knew he didn't expect one from her, but felt the silence weigh heavy between them. The only way she could prove love would stay would be to fall in love with him herself and stay with him all their lives. But who could live with unrequited love?

"Want to dance?" he asked.

Her mind in turmoil, she wanted to say no. To demand he give her a good reason why he doubted the bride and groom would stay together. But the music changed and a slow and sensual Miles Davis tune came on. She couldn't resist Preston or Miles Davis.

She nodded and stood. He took her arm to lead her to the dance floor. His fingers brushed on the inside, teasing her with their light touch. Her sleeveless sundress was light and flirty, a gauzy fabric that made her feel like a princess.

Her heels gave a few added inches but Preston still topped her. He pulled her into his arms. His lake-gray eyes weren't cold now. In fact, she saw fire reflected in their depths and wanted…wanted things she knew better than to ask for.

She rested her head against his shoulder to escape his probing gaze. He saw too much. Made her see herself in a new light, and she wasn't ready to look that closely at herself. Wasn't ready to acknowledge that something had to be missing for her to have caved so easily to Preston's advances. She'd stayed celibate a long time, but suddenly she wished she hadn't.

Because the man rubbing her back and cradling her against his body was special to her…more than she was to him, and Lily knew she wouldn't let her first time be with someone to whom she meant little or nothing. For her, firsts were celebrations.

His lips rested against her temple as they danced, and he talked quietly to her. Telling her how exciting it was to hold her in his arms, seducing her slowly with his words and body. She closed her eyes and let her senses revel in Preston Dexter—a man who no longer seemed like a cold man in pursuit of seduction. When the song ended, and they returned to their seats, he still felt unsteady.

Preston reluctantly joined Lily on the dance floor for a more rousing number. Cousins and friends surrounded her, and she threw her head back laughing as they danced around her. He felt the familiar tension pool in his lower body and didn't fight his reaction.

He'd been hard since he'd taken Lily in his arms on the dance floor an hour earlier. Though he'd always enjoyed the game of seduction and teasing, he was ready to have her in his bed. But he wasn't ready for her to be out of his life.

As she twirled past him in the arms of one of her beefy cousins, their eyes met and something magical passed between them. Preston stopped in the middle of the floor aware that everyone else still teemed around him. The world narrowed to only him and Lily. Seducing Lily had always been his goal, his objective, but he'd found himself losing sight of that.

Suddenly he realized that Lily was seducing him with her smiles and laughter, with the joy she found in everyday life that he never knew existed. He cut in and took her in his arms, dancing to the loud wild music as if he'd been born to it. He forgot about love and lust and let the music sweep both him and Lily away.

He let it play over him like his first illegal sip of whisky when he'd been fourteen. It was hard going down but the rush that came after thrilled him to his toes, and he knew he'd have to have another hit.

When the music stopped his ears were ringing. Lily was smiling up at him. The room was hot and close with the press of bodies, and he tugged on her hand, leading her outside. A naked bulb illuminated a rough path down to the waterfront.

Lily took his hand and led him down it. The moon was bright and full lighting their way. The music from the hall started again, fainter as they moved away. The smell of overripe vegetation and fresh water filled the air. The small canal flowed steadily toward the sea, and a wooden dock emerged from the shadows as they approached the bank.

"I haven't danced like that in ages," Lily said.

She seemed like an enchanted being from another world. One who would inhabit the earth for only this one night. If he didn't capture her, hang on to her, she'd be gone forever.

"I never have," he admitted.

"You must have natural rhythm." She glanced up at him from under her lashes. It was a flirty look and it intensified the tightness in his lower body.

He hugged her to him. She smelled of her exertions and of the floral perfume she wore every day. The scent reminded him of the exotic orchids the gardener had cultivated in his childhood home.

"Ah, Preston, I missed you when you were gone."

I missed you, too. "I'm back now."

Her entire body quivered with excitement, probably from the wedding and the dancing. Preston wanted to feel that same energy coursing through him. He wanted to feel it coursing from her into him as he joined their bodies together.

Nothing else would suffice.

"Wasn't it romantic?"

"The wedding?"

"No, their first kiss. I've always dreamed of that kiss."

He realized that Lily might have had a little too much to drink because she would never reveal that much of herself to him. Her natural resistance was lowered, and he knew that he could, if he played his cards right, finally be successful in tempting her into his bed.

"What kind of kiss is that?"

"I don't know. Magical, I guess."

"How are my kisses?"

She smiled at him, sweetly seductive, and laid her head on his shoulder. "Yours are steamy and hot, promising forbidden pleasures."

"I'm ready to deliver on them."

"I know."

He brushed his lips softly against hers. He wanted to taste some of the magic that Lily thought came from true love. Preston was beginning to realize it came from true goodness. There was something special about the way he felt for Lily, and that bothered him.

She should be like every other woman in his life. She shouldn't make him hard with just a glance. She shouldn't make him laugh over the silly things that happened during the day. She shouldn't be lying so

trustingly in his arms, because he knew once he kissed
her he wouldn't be able to stop.

"Hey, they're getting ready to cut the cake," someone called from the doorway.

Preston pulled back, aware that he was riding the
razor's edge. He wouldn't take her in his arms again
and not make love to her.

He put his hand on her back and directed her toward
the hall. The music grew louder, and he heard laughter
from the open windows. "Thanks."

"No problem."

"Are you okay, Preston?"

"We need to talk tonight."

"Okay," she said, and she walked away. He took
his time following her. Making sure he didn't get back
in the hall until after the dancing had started up again.
He didn't want to see what Lily wanted in life. Didn't
want to acknowledge what he knew deep in his soul—
that she deserved her Prince Charming. She deserved
her wedding and her groom, and he wasn't the man for
either of those roles.

Lily leaned dreamily against the plush leather seat
as Preston piloted the car through the late-evening traffic. It grew increasingly heavy as they neared the city.
New Orleans never slept, and for once Lily didn't want
to, either.

Her body still pulsed in time to the Cajun music
from the reception. Her mind still dwelled on the fantasy of herself as bride and her groom none other than

her sophisticated companion tonight. She hummed a nameless tune.

She slipped a CD she'd given him into the player. A Lena Horne disc of love songs. The sweet and sometimes bittersweet lyrics brushed over her aroused senses like moonlight on the ocean. She turned to her side, watching Preston in the flickering light provided by the passing streetlamps. He looked alone and aloof.

She wanted to penetrate the aura of loneliness that surrounded him, but how could she. How could she? She wasn't sure of anything any longer, especially love. Never had she backed down from anything in her life. Never had she had so much at stake, and for the soul of her she couldn't be sure of winning.

"What are you thinking?" he asked, his voice a husky rasp.

"Can I drive your car?" she asked, not wanting to open up her soul to him tonight. On the dance floor he'd felt like Prince Charming and she'd known exactly how Cinderella felt but now she wasn't so sure.

"Not tonight," he said, with a wry chuckle.

"No, not tonight," she agreed. She still had a pleasant buzz from the reception and the alcohol she'd consumed.

"Are these new CDs helping you to believe in love?" she asked.

He glanced at her as he coasted to a halt for a red light. "I wish they were."

"Don't you feel seduced by the promise of love?"

"Not especially."

''What would it take to seduce you, Preston?''

She watched him closely. She wanted him: his hard body and supple strength; his cold gray eyes sweeping over her feminine body; his warm touch spreading over her and bringing to life longings that only he could fill.

He pulled into her drive and turned off the engine. Her house, draped in darkness, should have been forbidding, but it looked the way it always did—a safe haven. She'd never ventured from her safe neighborhood. Part of her had longed to when she was younger, but as an adult she knew she never would.

The CD continued to play. Lena sang ''At Long Last Love.'' This song broke her heart. Lily didn't want to listen to it because sometimes she felt as if this might be her. Searching fruitlessly for something ephemeral that she'd never find.

''Invite me in and I'll tell you,'' Preston said.

Tell me what? she thought. Then she remembered. He'd tell her what it took to seduce him. She had bought a book of quotes the other day and planned to inundate him with words on the subject but not tonight. To bring love to his life she knew she'd have to risk herself, and suddenly the risk seemed worth the pain that might come.

''Come in?'' she asked, teasing him with a look from under her lashes. She knew then that she wanted to be seduced. That she wanted him to deliver on the forbidden treasures his kisses and eyes promised. Tonight, at least, that seemed enough.

''Yes, angel.''

He came around and helped her out of the car. His hand was solid and sure at her elbow. Heat spread up the inside of her bare flesh, tightening her breast and bringing her nipples to an aching point.

The moonlight played over his chiseled features. There was nothing soft about Preston, and in the shadows he lost the facade of civilization that he wore, day in and day out.

She swallowed. This man, who was more at home in darkness than in light, was the one who'd challenged her to teach him to love and didn't believe she could achieve it.

She led him into her house. The light she'd left on in the parlor spilled onto the hardwood floor in the hallway. She hesitated when she entered the room and saw the books she'd left perched on the end table. Books about love and its celebration. She led Preston to the love seat farthest from the books. Maybe he wouldn't notice.

Good manners demanded she offer him a drink, but she knew if she left the room he'd find those books, and she wasn't ready to discuss love tonight. Not tonight, because it might spoil the mood that permeated through her like the champagne had at the wedding. The intimate setting of Preston's plush car and the mellow music had made her want to live in the bubble of intimacy, even if it wasn't real.

"Let's talk seduction," she said, sliding closer to him on the love seat. He'd left his jacket in the car, and his body heat drew her closer. Her thin dress was adequate for the temperature outside, but inside it suddenly didn't seem enough. She put her hand on his thigh and teased herself with the image of his naked leg beneath her pink-tipped fingernails.

"I don't think an expert like you needs to discuss anything," he said with a pointed glance at her hand on his thigh.

She was in a mood to tease him. The way he'd been when she'd dined at his apartment. She slid one finger up the inside of his thigh. "Expert?"

He covered her hand with his own. "Of course. Don't push me too far, Lily."

"I'm sorry." She slid her hand out from under his, feeling more and more like someone she didn't know.

"What do you want from me?" he asked.

She didn't know. Part of her wanted to believe he could be that man she'd been waiting for all of her life, but another part didn't want to leave herself open to the vulnerability that would bring. "I'm the novice here. I'm the one searching for love."

"But you're seducing me into believing that myth, as well."

"It's only seduction if it's against your best wishes."

"It is," he said with a finality that should have made her leap from the couch and kick him out of her house. But she sensed the fear under the words. Someone had taught Preston that loving was weak and brought only pain. It was up to her to show him the real value in it. Was Preston vulnerable, too?

"What would it take to seduce you, Preston Dexter?"

"Tonight?"

She nodded.

"A bit of that magic you mentioned earlier."

She blinked against the emotion swamping her. "Come here."

He leaned closer. She pulled him into her arms and into an embrace that brought them body to body, that let her touch her lips to his. She tried to bring the magic that had been surrounding her all her life to him.

Preston took control of the kiss with a harsh groan. His grip on her shoulders tightened, and his mouth slanted on hers. His tongue penetrated deeply, as if trying to learn the taste of her completely. He tasted of the coffee he'd had before they left the reception and of something undefinable that was only Preston.

She thrust her tongue into his mouth, trying to assuage a thirst that had sprung from nowhere and wouldn't be stopped. She didn't know where the line between seducer and seduced had ended but suddenly that didn't matter. She only knew that having Preston in her arms was where he belonged. He always seemed so cold and lonely, except when she tempted him into her arms.

Seven

Preston had never craved anything as much as he craved Lily's body under his. He wanted to sheath his throbbing erection in her warm, welcoming body. To see if she'd deliver on the promises her eyes had been making all night.

He'd been wrong to make any sort of dare with her. Success lay in the familiar. He bent to nibble on her neck as she leaned back against the cushions of the sofa. There was something vulnerable about the curve of a woman's neck, and Lily's seemed more so. Though he wanted to stop and caress it with his fingertips, to touch her as he would something fragile, he didn't.

He smoothed his mouth to her ear and whispered

dark promises to her. She shifted restlessly on the couch. Her eyes half-lidded as her hands grasped at his shoulders and tried to pull him closer. But he knew the only type of closeness that would satisfy them both was naked flesh to naked flesh.

He couldn't give her magic, but he could give her passion. It was the one area of his life where he'd always excelled. He'd never had any trouble mastering his body and his reactions to women. At an early age he'd learned the game of seduction.

Lily's hands found his head, and she pulled his mouth to hers. She wasn't grasping in her desire but welcoming. She wanted him and wanted him to want her. *As if he didn't.*

It felt he'd wanted her forever. Blood pounded through his veins like the rush he got when driving his Jag wide open on a deserted highway with no care given to speed limits or safety. He never let himself dwell too long on the man he was then because that man didn't know how to survive in the real world.

Lily brushed her lips to his, barely touching them. Back and forth until he thought he would completely lose control. He held her head still in his grasp, needing to be inside at least her mouth. But he felt the challenge she'd thrown down as clearly as if she'd waved a red flag in front of his face. That kiss of hers had been a provocation. And he called on the skills he'd honed on faceless women from his past to entice her now.

He bent to her, but she slid back from the kiss and nibbled instead on his lower lip. The world narrowed, and only one person existed. The exhalation of her breath seemed loud in the silent room. His thundering heartbeat steadily drowned out the sound. He had to have her.

He sucked her upper lip into his mouth and Lily moaned. ''Oh, Pres…''

He remembered how shy and tentative she'd been the first time he'd embraced her. She'd grown bolder, and Preston reveled in her reactions to him. The one time men and women were most honest with each other was in a physically intimate situation.

He took possession of her mouth, molding it to his own, thrusting his tongue past the barrier of her teeth as he caressed his way down her body with his hands. She rubbed her tongue against his, and he shifted on the couch, bringing Lily onto his lap.

Her full breasts rose and fell with each breath she took. The light from the lamp cast a soft glow in the room, but Preston wished it were brighter. He wanted to see the body he was caressing. He wanted to know if her breasts were pink tipped, as he imagined, if her hair were red everywhere and if she'd let him stare at her until they both felt as if they'd go up in flames.

He teased her with a circling touch around her breast, confirming what he'd suspected earlier—she wasn't wearing a bra. Just the tiniest light caress, knowing she wanted—needed—more from him.

But he wanted this to last forever. Suddenly it was important that she experience satisfaction. He needed to watch her blossom in his arms. And she was doing so, beautifully.

Her nipple hardened under his stroking finger and he had to taste it. He tugged her forward. Her hands kneaded his shoulders and then she scraped her fingernails down his back, following the line of his spine.

With a firm touch between her shoulderblades Preston brought her chest in alignment with his mouth. He suckled her through the layer of her thin dress. She moaned and her hands clutched at his head. Preston sucked harder, trying to pull a response from her that would match the one pulsing through his body.

Her legs straddled his hips, and through the thin layer of her dress he felt her feminine warmth. His fingers tingled to touch her. To feel her honey spilling on his fingers. He wanted to open his fly and feel that warmth on his engorged flesh but knew better. He didn't want this to end yet.

He was so hard, he could scarcely breathe. Yet he couldn't pull away from the temptation of her body. He turned his attention to her other breast. Lily's hands roamed over his back searchingly.

He wanted her long fingers on his flesh but didn't have the patience to remove his shirt. Her hips rocked against his groin. Sliding his hands up under her dress, he took the taut globes of her butt in his hands, fondling her through her lace panties. She gasped and rocked harder against him.

''Preston?'' her high questioning sound drew his attention.

"It's okay, angel."

She was on the knife's edge and he realized that she'd never been there before. How innocent was she? His body didn't care, but his conscience nagged. He slid his palm around to cup her feminine heat. She was as warm and tempting as he'd imagined but there was more. He found the center of her excitement and teased it gently with his finger until she couldn't stay still. She brought her mouth to his and as he slid his tongue deep into her recesses, he entered her body with first one finger and then, stretching her gently, added another.

Her body was warm and tight, sheathing his fingers like a warm glove. He almost lost it right then, imagining her tight warmth on his erection. He thrust deeper into her body and watched her arch in response. He knew he couldn't stop now. Wouldn't be able to stop until he was hilt deep, surrounded by her tight heat and the warmth that came only from Lily.

"Oh, Preston, what's happening?"

"Just ride it out, angel."

She did—beautifully so. Arching against him, holding her body tight until tiny contractions tightened her even more around his fingers. Before falling against his shoulder, her uneven breathing filling the silent room.

Preston was rock hard and wanted nothing more than to slip into her body. But he realized there were consequences to this that he'd never thought of before. Consequences that hadn't ever existed in his world until now. "Lily, are you a virgin?"

She snuggled closer to him, burying her face against his chest. "Yes."

The White Willow House was slowly returning to the splendor it had enjoyed in its pre-Civil War era. Some of the antiques she'd ordered from France and Spain had started arriving. She'd hired a local artisan to craft replicas for each of the guest rooms. Lily knew she'd done her best work yet.

She'd neglected some of her other clients to concentrate on the Dexter Resorts project. And she'd been working long days to make up for it. Which was just as well, because in the two weeks since she'd confessed to being a virgin, Preston had left her alone.

Part of her, the Catholic girl who'd gone to confession once a week, was glad. But in her heart she wanted to experience Preston as only a woman could. He made the world seem brighter and life more…exciting and interesting.

She wondered if he thought he might catch it from her. Always willing to go to the wall to win, she hadn't let his busy schedule detract from her campaign to convince him love existed. Last night she'd sent him two e-mails and a fax with some quotes she'd unearthed.

He hadn't responded. But he'd sent a thank-you note for the basket of romantic CDs and DVDs that she'd had delivered on Monday. Twilight cast long shadows on the hardwood floors of the suite she'd just added a candelabra to. She imagined how it must have been to live in the days of candlelight. When everything was a little softer.

She imagined a Mozart waltz floating upstairs from the ballroom through the open window and bowed to an imaginary partner, then waltzed around the room.

Someone cleared his throat and she turned guiltily toward the open door. Preston stood in the shadows like a vampire afraid of the light of day. Embarrassed, she put her hand to her throat and looked around for her planner. He looked tired, she thought. As if he was running from something that was gaining on him.

She longed to open her arms and offer him the solace of her body, but she was afraid she'd be left a shell of a woman when he moved on. She wanted him to realize what a precious gift they had been given because she'd come to know that Preston was her soul mate. He looked to the future while she fixed the past. Together they both brought things to each other that neither could live without.

"Don't stop on my account." His voice brushed over her senses. That deep husky sound that brought back the last time she heard it. On her love seat two weeks ago. Two long weeks ago. Her heartbeat had doubled and blood rushed to the center of her body.

"It was a private show." She gathered her stuff and walked toward him. He blocked the doorway with his body. She realized how tall he was for the first time. Maybe it was because she was wearing Keds instead of her work boots.

He raised one eyebrow. "I'm very discriminating."

That he was. Plus he played his cards so close to his chest no one had any idea what he was thinking. "I know."

"So dance for me."

She was tempted because she knew it would give him pleasure, and Preston seemed to have too little of that in his life. But he had to learn that she wasn't an oddity in his life. She wasn't a new toy that could be taken out and played with when he was bored. She was a real woman and deserved to be treated as such by him. "Preston, I'm not one of your flunkies. You can't avoid me for two weeks, then expect me to do whatever you ask."

"I've been busy."

"You're the boss. You could rearrange your schedule." But she knew he wouldn't. She'd realized when he'd disappeared the last time that when emotions started to affect him, Preston backed away and regrouped, coming back stronger and more resolute in the confidence that love didn't exist.

"I don't think of you as one of my flunkies."

"What do you think of me?" she asked, realizing she might not like the answer.

"The woman who's going to teach me to love."

It may have been a little thing, but for the first time he hadn't said to convince him love existed. He'd said to teach him to love. Appealing to his mind was a tack that might convince him. Because beyond the monetary, she'd discovered that Preston liked things he could take apart and figure out how they worked. Like that expensive car of his. He knew it inside and out.

"Did you like the Balzac quote?"

"Which one was it?"

"'Love is to the mortal nature what the sun is to the earth.'" It was one of her favorites, and she'd spent a lot of time finding just the right quote for him.

"Not particularly. The sun is eating through more of the ozone layer each year and bringing us closer to death."

Sometimes he tried her patience. "The sun warms us in winter and gives us food in spring and summer."

"You believe love provides that?"

"It provides the foundation for a happy life."

"It also has that rare side effect of tearing someone's life to shreds."

She shook her head. "For every one person burned by love there are ten more who rejoice in it."

"Some people live their entire lives without love."

"Because they are afraid of it."

"Are you calling me a coward?"

"No, I wasn't thinking of you at all." But she had been. He frustrated her sometimes, and her good nature only lasted so long.

"I think you were. You didn't really wound me," he said, but his eyes told another story. She forgot that Preston was good at hiding his real emotions, and she had lashed out when she shouldn't have. She'd known from the beginning that he'd be a tough nut to crack.

"I haven't given up on you yet," she said.

"You will."

His quiet confidence unnerved her, and she walked out of the room afraid to say anything else. But her heart was weary and her body was aching. Her instincts told her that if she was alone with him again, his belief in love might not matter to her body.

"How's your wife, Jay?" Lily asked. They were sitting in one of the three gazebos that were behind White Willow House. It overlooked a man-made lake that Preston planned to stock with bass and offer water-skiing and fishing trips to his guests.

Lily had brought lunch back for the crew from town when she'd arrived with another truckload of antiques. The weekend had passed with lots of attempts on Lily's part to involve him in her life, but Preston had remained resolute.

She was so open and friendly that he wasn't surprised she knew about Rohr's wife. Nor did it surprise him that she'd taken the time to bring po' boy sandwiches for the crew. That was the kind of thing that Lily did.

Because she cared, he realized.

"Well, we're in the homestretch. Thanks for those books you recommended," Jay Rohr said. Jay was one of the most competent of Dexter's vice presidents. He'd been with Preston from the beginning and though only two years older, Jay had been a mentor to Preston those first few years when he had more gumption than know-how.

"Homestretch of what, Rohr?" Preston asked. He vaguely recalled Rohr's wife, a brown-haired woman who was as tall as Jay. They'd married a year and a half ago. Rohr hadn't taken a vacation since his marriage.

Lily stared pointedly at him. The dappled sun made her red hair shine. "June's pregnancy."

Preston realized that Lily knew his people better than he did. It had never bothered him before and wouldn't now if he hadn't realized that Lily had found him lacking. He didn't care what type of life his employees had away from the office. "Is that why you requested she accompany you down here?"

"Yes. June asked me to be active in the birthing."

"How?" Preston asked. There was only so much a man could do.

"I asked the same thing. She wants me to be coaching her. I can't explain it, but it makes her feel better to see me every night."

Preston had no idea what else to say. None of his friends had kids or even wanted them. But as Lily picked up the conversation turning it away from Rohr's upcoming fatherhood, he realized that the thought of Lily pregnant wasn't an unwelcome one. Dammit, of course it was, he reminded himself.

But his mind lingered on the image of her swollen with his seed. Her hands cradling her belly while his child rested, safe within her womb.

"Preston?" Lily said, drawing his attention.

"What?" He didn't want to be a father. He wanted

Lily in his bed for the normal male reasons. Lust, desire and, well, affection. But he didn't want a future with her or any other woman.

"Jay married his wife for love," she said, with a smile that shot straight to his groin. He'd been walking around aroused for weeks and knew he was reaching the point where he'd have to take Lily to bed or leave entirely. He didn't trust himself in this mood. His control was shaky and his emotions were in turmoil.

"You don't say," Preston said, dryly. He knew for a fact that Rohr loved his job more than any woman— even a wife.

"No, he does."

"Only love, Rohr?" Jay straightened his tie and stood up.

"No, sir."

"Oh, really, Jay," Lily said as if she were heartbroken to hear the news.

"Sorry, Lily. June married me to escape her family. There were pressuring her to join the family law firm, and she wanted to be a housewife. So she made me an offer I couldn't refuse."

Preston bet the offer involved sex but hoped Jay knew enough not to say that to Lily. She had some strange notions about men and women but he didn't want her disillusioned. That was the reason he'd returned every night to his cold, dark apartment, his body tormented by the memories of her in his arms.

"Do you love her now?" she asked.

"More than life itself."

Preston felt a little sorry for Rohr and doubted the man knew what to say when Lily was questioning him the way a marine corps drill sergeant would a new recruit.

"I better be getting back to the office. I have a conference call in forty-five minutes with the Italians on that marble you wanted."

Jay left, and Preston watched Lily tidy up her lunch bag and then pat her hair as if afraid a lock was out of place.

"Just because Jay didn't marry for love doesn't mean he wasn't in love with her."

"I think he was in lust with her."

"Really. Do you think men focus on lust because it's safer?"

"I don't know. I do know that most of the men I know who are married are always vague about how they ended up in that state."

"Do you think they were brainwashed, Pres?"

"No, I just think they wouldn't have chosen to be there."

"They weren't forced to marry."

"Who says a woman didn't use emotional blackmail or maybe the enticement of a child."

"Would that be enough for you? A child?"

"Hell, no. I'd be a lousy father but some men want to pass on their names."

"You don't?"

"I want the Dexter name to stand for first-class resort hotels. I'm not too concerned about a Preston, Jr., running around.''

"Children are the future."

"I live in the present," he said.

"Sooner or later we all have to look forward."

"I do, just not personally."

"Why not?"

"What will be will be."

Lily didn't say anything else, but he knew his life purpose differed greatly from hers. "If you decide to be with me in a relationship, Lily, it will be for now. For as long as we both are happy together."

"Do I make you happy, Pres?"

He stared out across the lake and saw not the leisure boaters who'd bring him revenue but Lily and a small family picnicking on a sailboat.

"Preston?"

"Yes," he said, standing up and walking away from both the woman and the image.

Eight

Watching Preston walk away, Lily knew that she wasn't going to convince him love existed without loving him completely. He needed to experience it and learn to recognize it. Her feelings for him had been steadily increasing since the night they'd almost made love, and for once in her life she was ready to gamble. Ready for the adventure that seemed always on a distant horizon. But habits were hard to break, and she admitted to herself that she was afraid of getting hurt.

"Preston?"

He stopped outside the gazebo. Lily leaned over one of the walls so that she was closer to him. "Don't run away."

He pivoted on his heel, facing her with the pent-up

fury of a god who'd been defied. She'd been playing with fire without even realizing it. He was a dangerous man, but because she'd cared for him, she'd never noticed.

"Lily, I'm damned tired of you accusing me of being a coward."

"I'm not."

"It sure sounds that way. I'm a man people are afraid of."

"I understand," she said, and for the first time she really did. If she was confused by what was happening between them, Preston would be doubly so. Lily had always believed in happy endings. He thought anyone who did was a few bricks short of a load.

"When I walk away from you, angel, it's so that I won't ruin your rose-colored vision of the world."

That hurt. "I've seen plenty of reality."

"Then where is the realism that comes with it?" He stalked closer to her. The white wood barrier of the gazebo was a scant one. She wanted to shrink away from him but at the same time was drawn closer.

"I don't have to be cynical to have experienced pain."

"No, but you should be practical enough to avoid the same situation."

"What are you talking about?" she asked.

"The truth you keep harping on."

"What truth?" She feared his answer. Preston's cold gray eyes were harder than the glaciers of the North Atlantic.

"That you haven't been embracing love but hiding from it."

Lily was stunned and silent. Was that true? She'd been busy the past few years. She'd never hidden from love, because she wanted to experience the beauty her parents had.

"You've used your brothers for an excuse to keep men at bay for the past few years, and now you're using devotion as a reason to keep me away."

"I'm not." But Lily doubted herself for the first time. There was some truth to what he'd said. She'd never let anyone close to her after her parents' deaths. But she wanted Preston closer to her. She'd done everything she knew to get him to be her man, and he'd walked away.

"Then why do you keep tying us both up in knots? Why do you fight the one thing that would convince me you feel some sort of affection for me?"

"What thing?" she asked, fearing the answer.

"Intimacy."

"I don't fear it any more than you do."

"No, you just hide from it or run from it because you can't control it, Lily."

She had no answer for him. It was true she feared what Preston made her feel. Feared how out of his league she really was. Feared that she might never meet anyone again who would ever make her feel as alive as he did.

"I'm just—"

"Trying not to get hurt."

"Is that what *you've* been doing? Is that why you always walk away when I get too close?"

"Yes."

The sincerity in his voice struck straight through to her heart. Preston knew what she felt because he felt some of it, too. He walked away again, and this time she didn't stop him.

Her emotions ricocheted through her like an out-of-control electrical wire. She wanted Preston with a passion that had to be experienced to be believed. But she liked him, too. The little idiosyncrasies that made him human. The things that the society pages never covered. Like his obsession with his car and his thirst for winning. The way he could make her see a side of life that she'd always trivialized.

Maybe it was time for another quote. She'd had greater success with them than with any of the real couples she'd introduced him to. Reaching into her purse, she pulled out the small book she'd been using as her main source. Thumbing through the pages she stood stock-still as she realized the answer was in her hands. Staring her in the eye as it were. A quote by Hannah More: "Love never reasons, but profusely gives, like a thoughtless prodigal, it's all, and trembles then lest it has done so little."

She closed her eyes and repeated the quote to herself. It felt like the answer but she wasn't sure that it was. She had to give to Preston to make him realize that love existed. *Give to Preston....*

She gathered up the remains of their lunch and

walked slowly back to the main house. She had no idea how to convince Preston. But she knew protestations of love weren't going to get it done. It was going to take more than she'd ever given a man before. She wondered if being a virgin was going to hamper her efforts at breaking through the wall that Preston used to protect himself from the world.

Part of his problems lay in the past. She'd have to be blind not to notice the way he focused only in the now. She didn't want to fix his life. She just wanted to find a way for them both to be happy. Find a place where they'd both be comfortable. She wasn't ready to give her body and not her heart.

Seduction was the key, she realized. She'd have to plan carefully. She'd use everything at her disposal to convince him to love her. Frankly she was afraid to move forward, but she wasn't one to back down from a challenge and Preston was right: it was time to face *intimacy*.

Preston stared out the floor-to-ceiling windows that lined the general manager's office at White Willow House. He'd claimed the office as his own while the project was still in the production phase. The sun sank below the horizon and darkness fell. In the distance the Crescent City lights beckoned, promising revelry to all who entered its streets.

He hadn't been this tense since Dexter Resorts had gone public his second year at the helm. The White Willow House was progressing on schedule, but his life was careening out of control. Everything he'd ever taken for granted now seemed different. For the first time ever he wanted to talk to someone, but he didn't know whom to turn to.

He'd insulated himself from those around him so thoroughly that he'd never noticed the silence before. Never noticed the polite chitchat that masqueraded as conversation. New Orleans pulsed around him with a life force of its own. For once he wasn't out enjoying the nightlife and the endless round of women it offered a man in his position.

The office door creaked open.

"You're here late," said Lily.

He watched her reflection in the plate-glass window. She looked pale and withdrawn. He'd almost sent her a dozen roses as an apology for his words yesterday afternoon, but if he apologized she'd realize how much she was coming to mean to him. And he couldn't let that happen. He wouldn't depend on anyone for anything.

He'd never been tempted to. Not since he was eight and his world had been shifted irreversibly. He'd done a good job at keeping his distance from many people. How had one small woman slipped through?

"You look so lonely tonight," Lily said. He heard her footsteps and watched in the glass as she came closer to him. The light from the room shone through her thin cotton dress revealing her curvy female body.

He didn't know if it was emotion he was battling or his conscience. Because he knew that he wanted her even if she was a virgin. He wanted to peel away the layers she kept between herself and the world and find the real Lily, the one he'd hurt yesterday. Then he wanted to put her back together again.

"Preston?" She brushed her hand down his sleeve, stopping at his palm. Her long cool fingers gently caressing.

He grunted. Words were beyond him. He wanted her with the same soul-searching devotion that a preacher had to save sinners' eternal lives. At that moment he shook with the need to pull her into his arms. To feel her mouth under his and tangle his tongue with hers. To press her soft body to his harder one until there were no lines left where he ended and she began.

"I'm sorry I let things go too far the other day," she said. He knew he should say something, but he couldn't concentrate. Her scent assailed him. Flowers and *Lily*. She smelled distinctly like woman. Not something that could be manufactured and bottled but an essence that spoke straight to his hormones and sent his testosterone level skyrocketing.

Blood rushed through him, hardening his groin. He wanted to move his legs, to shift his position, but she was too close. If he moved, he'd take her. Sweep her up over his shoulder and not stop until they reached his desk. He'd push that flimsy skirt to her waist and rip her panties out of his way. Then he'd slide home. *Yes, home.* He needed to be inside her and feel her wrapped all around him. Clinging to him as he moved with fierce thrusts until she exploded for him again.

"Preston, I've been thinking about something."

He had no idea what she was talking about, only knew that he had to move away from her. Had to put some distance between them or he'd give in to his instincts. Yet his feet felt rooted to the ground.

"Preston, what is wrong with you?" she asked, cupping his face in her palm.

"Don't touch me," he ground out. It had been too long since he'd had a woman. Too long since he'd wanted any woman except Lily, and frankly he didn't want to wait another night. But she deserved better than him for her first experience in the sensual arts. She deserved a man who could love her. A man who'd take that trip down the aisle with her.

"Sorry." She took a half step away from him. Her eyes met his in the glass window, and she flinched. A telltale sheen of tears glittered in her eyes.

He knew he was hurting her again. Why did that keep happening? He was trying so hard to protect her from the beast he knew lurked beneath the sophisticated man he presented to the world. Why did she keep coming back to him with her soft touches and kind words?

"Lily, this has to stop."

"I don't understand. You challenged me to make you believe in love."

"I want you in my bed. That was the reason for the challenge."

"I wasn't saying no after the wedding reception."

"Well, you should have been."

"Why? Because I'm a virgin."

He glanced at her, no longer trusting the distorted image in the glass. "Yes."

"I think I'm big enough to make my own decisions." He let his gaze sweep over her body, and it inflamed the fire already running through his veins. She was his dream woman, he realized. Nice-size breasts, long slender legs and that short, sassy red hair that framed her angelic features.

"Sure you are, but I'm the one who'll have to deal with the consequences when you believe that you've traded your body for love."

"I know better than that. I'm the one who's been trying for weeks to convince you love is real."

"Don't trust me, Lily."

"Why not?"

"I want you too badly now to play fair. So here's your warning, angel. Leave now or stay and pay the consequences."

"What consequences?"

"Gamble with that sweet body of yours."

She paled but didn't walk away. He admired her spirit but wanted to warn her to not let every damned thing she felt show on her face. He should walk away. He should return to Manhattan and let Rohr finish this project or head to Barbados so that Lily wouldn't tempt him.

She stood poised, ready like a rabbit to run from a predator. He knew one wrong word would send her flying from him. And he knew that he should be saying that wrong word and sending her away.

One right word would make her stay.

He had no right, but he wanted what others took for granted. He wanted what he'd seen her give to her customers, friends and family. He wanted to bask in her light and wallow in her purity. He wanted...Lily.

"Lily, please."

"Please, what?"

"Stay with me."

She bit her lip and looked around the rather sparse office. The desk that he'd imagined taking her on was a sleek mahogany that would have tempted a more experienced woman. The floors were cold hard marble, and the only chair, a big leather executive model.

"Here?" she asked. She was game but scared.

Because he wasn't going to be her forever man, Preston knew he had to make Lily's first time special. Not some hurried coupling in his office.

"No, not here. And not tonight. Spend this weekend with me on my yacht. We'll go out on the Gulf. Just the two of us."

She took a deep breath. He hoped she didn't change her mind or he'd have to resort to that damned desk.

"Okay."

Relief coursed through him, and he wanted to pull her into his arms, but he'd wait until they could really be alone to make love to Lily.

Preston hadn't spoken to her for two days. He'd sent flowers, champagne and a negligee that would've made an experienced woman blush. Lily, though excited about her weekend with Preston, was ready to back out. Suddenly she didn't know if loving him would be enough. And how she would protect herself if it turned out he couldn't love her.

She'd phoned her brothers and grandmother and told them she'd be out of town for the weekend. They'd been surprised that she was going anywhere but hadn't asked whom she was going with. As if they'd believe she was spending the weekend on a yacht with a man. She was living it and hardly believed it.

Mae had offered her practical advice—don't let him know how much you care. But Lily didn't know how to lie like that. Didn't know how to protect herself from the one thing she wanted most in the world. Preston Dexter.

A sleek, black limousine pulled up in front of her house. Lily nervously wondered if he expected her to make love in the back seat with him. She'd heard stories of people doing those kinds of things. But she'd never once imagined it.

Oh, God, she thought, I can't do this.

Preston had been right. She was afraid of intimacy. Afraid that she'd lose again the way she had when her parents died and her world had been shattered. She'd built a safe haven for herself where nothing but pre-dictability ruled.

Preston emerged from the car, dark glasses covering his eyes, his Armani suit fitting his frame perfectly. He moved up the walk like a man who ruled the world, and Lily realized he ruled her heart. He hesitated on the walkway. Turned as if he was going to get back in the limo and leave.

Seeing Preston's indecision forced her to open the door. She wanted Preston in her life. She wanted him enough to take risks.

"Pres?"

He strode to her with the smooth determination she'd always known him to possess. If she hadn't seen him from her window she wouldn't have suspected he'd hesitated. She wanted to ask him what he'd been waiting for, but he didn't give her a chance.

"Ready to go, angel?"

"Yes," she said, but her answer sounded weak to her ears. She knew that one of the reasons Preston had been drawn to her from the beginning was that she'd met him as an equal. She had to do so now. She wasn't normally a cowering type and didn't plan to start now.

"Yes, I am," she said again. This time, though, the words were for her. She was going to win their challenge, because neither of them would be satisfied with anything less. Her heart's desire now seemed twined to Preston, and her future seemed less exciting without him in it.

"Where's your suitcase?" he asked.

"In the hall. Having never been on an illicit weekend before I wasn't sure what to pack. I picked up a magazine that advertised 'What to Wear to Tempt Your Man.'"

"Then we won't need your suitcase. Because nothing is exactly what you should be wearing."

She blushed. She knew they'd have to be naked, and she wanted to see Preston's body and to feel him moving over her. But she was uncomfortable in her own skin. It had been different after Marti and Brad's wedding, because there had been magic in the air, but today, standing in the front yard of the house she'd lived in all her life, she felt a little too ordinary for Preston.

"You can seduce me without even trying, angel," he said, his voice a husky rasp. He brushed one finger along her chin and then cupped her head and brought her closer for a kiss. He rubbed his lips briefly over hers and pulled back before she'd had a chance to reciprocate.

"You, too," she said, with a shy smile.

"So what'd you pack?" he asked, picking up her suitcases.

"A swimsuit."

"Well, there goes my fantasy. That must be one big suit."

"Maybe one or two other little things."

"The negligee?"

"You'll have to wait and see."

"I've been fantasizing about that damned lingerie since I saw it in the catalog."

"I might not look as glamorous as the model did. You know I think they airbrush their bodies—"

Preston's finger over her lips stopped the flow of words that her nervous system kept feeding her.

"I know that you won't look like they did."

She swallowed against the disappointment. Of course reality dictated that she wasn't going to be able to compete with an underwear model, but she would have liked to cling to the illusion that he found her sexy despite the fact that she was a rather ordinary girl-next-door type.

"You're going to put her to shame."

She glanced up at him and saw herself reflected in the dark lenses of his glasses. Without thinking, she removed his glasses. Sincerity and some other emotion, something she couldn't define but that warmed her to her toes shone there.

She knew then that she was meant to be Preston's woman. That he made her stronger than she could be on her own. And she had the power to do the same to him. But he wasn't looking for the future, and when Lily looked at him, stared deep into his beautiful gray eyes, she saw them growing old together.

Nine

Preston had never had a woman on the yacht before. He used it mainly for business deals. In fact, it felt odd to have only Lily with him on the yacht. When he entertained, he had a crew of five who catered to the whims of his business associates. Since they were only cruising out in the Gulf, Preston dismissed the staff and asked only the captain and chef to remain onboard the *Gold Digger*. His father had named the yacht after his third wife had left him.

He carried Lily's suitcases into the master stateroom and felt her following closely behind. She was nervous, and he wanted her so badly. He was tempted to pull her into his arms and soothe her with kisses. But the bed was only five steps away. And the floor covered with thick rich carpets imported from Persia. If he started kissing her they'd spend the weekend docked instead of out on the sea. And he wanted more than that with Lily.

He glanced over his shoulder and found Lily with her shoes off and eyes closed. Her red-painted toenails burrowed into the thick carpet, and a small smile graced her face. She had a toe ring on her left foot, and Preston couldn't stop staring at it.

"Pres, this is great. How long have you had the yacht?"

All he could think about was that damned toe ring. He wanted to suckle her little toes. He wanted to feel the ring scraping along his calf as he made love to her.

"It was my dad's."

"I like it a lot. Is that a print?" she asked, pointing to the Gauguin oil above the bed.

"No. It's a bear to keep in good condition, but it really makes the room." Or so the decorator had told him.

"Who named the yacht?"

"Dear old Dad."

"I was afraid you'd named it." The way she watched him made him feel better than he was. Like he'd done something to deserve her trust and respect. He knew he hadn't.

"Nah, he did."

She walked closer to him and sat down on the bed. Preston's instincts screamed at him to push her back and settle himself over her. To take her lips in long, drugging kisses until they were away from the coast and out at sea.

"There's got to be a story behind it." She smiled at him, and his pulse increased. She went through his system faster than hundred-proof whisky. Her body was pressed against his and he felt each inhalation of breath through her body.

"Well, my dad had a lousy track record with women, and after his third divorce he bought this boat and named it *Gold Digger* to remind himself that all women were after only one thing."

She stared pensively away from him, and Preston realized how that would sound to her. The story had always seemed kind of funny to him as he'd been growing up. Even his mother had chuckled when she'd heard the name. But then, his mother was wealthy in her own right and hadn't married his father for money.

"Well, now I know where you got your theory on relationships."

"Lily, it doesn't mean anything. It's a joke." He tried to pull her closer. Brought his arms around her but she shifted subtly away from him.

"Yeah, I know. I guess I just don't get it."

She stood and started to walk away. He grabbed her wrist.

"Where are you going?"

"Um... I think I'll go up on deck while we leave the harbor. I've always loved the sea breezes."

She kept talking until she'd disappeared up the gangway. Damn. He'd hurt her again. Part of him realized that it might have been intentional. He knew that Lily wasn't after his money, but he wanted to hear her say it.

He left the cabin, found the captain and asked him to weigh anchor. He didn't want to lose Lily but didn't know how to undo the hurt he'd unwittingly inflicted. Ordinarily he wouldn't bother worry about it, but this was Lily and she mattered more to him than he wanted to acknowledge.

He grabbed a bottle of Dom from the galley and the fresh-cut strawberries he'd ordered left in there. The trappings of seduction. He hadn't thought he'd need them but now knew he did.

He found her on the aft deck sitting on one of the sun chairs. Large glasses covered her face and her hair whipped around her head. She lifted her face to the sun and took a deep breath as if she were trying to deal with some deep, tearing emotion. Had he done this to her?

He set the berries and champagne on the deck table and sat at her feet. Where he knew he belonged. Startled, she jerked upright and turned her face away.

"Angel, don't give up on me yet."

"I can't fight this, Preston."

"I'm not asking you to."

"No, you're not, but someday you're going to look at me and wonder if I'm staying with you because of your money."

"I won't," he said, but knew the words were a lie. No one had ever stayed except for money.

"Yes, you will. And you know it, don't you?"

"Maybe. It doesn't mean anything. I'll change the name of the damned boat."

"Can you change how you were raised?"

"No. Can you?"

"I don't want to. I don't believe everyone in the world who has less money than I do can be bought."

"I don't believe it, either. Not anymore." He still couldn't see her eyes and wasn't sure she trusted him. But it was the best he could do. Life had taught him some harsh lessons. And though Lily tied him in knots sexually, he wasn't sure he trusted what he felt for her.

He reached for the bottle of champagne and the long-stemmed flutes he brought with him. "I didn't ask you to spend this weekend fighting with me."

He handed the glasses to Lily. She hesitated, then, sighing, took them.

"And I didn't agree to come just to argue with you."

"Why did you agree?"

"For reasons you wouldn't believe."

"Don't be coy."

"I'm not. I never realized how hard winning that challenge was going to be until this moment."

He said nothing.

"I can't make you love," she said softly. He knew he should fill the void, give her something she needed from him, but he honestly didn't know how. Lily wanted something from him that he knew didn't exist. Now she knew it, too.

* * *

Preston suggested they go for a swim when they stopped in the early evening. There was no land in sight, only endless sea in every direction. Lily felt as if she and Preston were the only two people in the world. After their tense conversation she'd been afraid he'd pressure her into bed. In fact, she wasn't sure when they'd make love. She still wanted him with a fierce desire that sent her pulse racing whenever she looked at him, but she was leery of him emotionally.

Her battle to teach him to love kept encountering defenses that she'd never known existed. Like hidden land mines going off in peacetime, she thought.

Uncomfortable showing a lot of skin, she normally wore a very conservative one-piece suit, but Mae had taken her shopping, insisting she needed something flashier. So here she was donning a tiny two-piece affair that made her feel like… A glance in the mirror stopped that thought. Her body was revealed but she didn't look as bad as she'd imagined she would. In fact, the color brought out what was left of her tan, and the cut made her legs look longer than they really were.

For a moment she felt as if she belonged on this well-appointed yacht and with the wealthy man who owned it. The man who thought that naming a boat *Gold Digger* was a pretty funny joke. Despite what he'd said, she felt he'd been sending her a message. And she knew there was no way she'd ever have enough money for him to believe that his didn't matter to her.

She pushed that thought away. This might be the

only chance she had with Preston. The only way to convince him love really existed. She'd prepared a few little notes and gifts for him. Really small things, but he was important to her and she didn't give herself lightly. She needed to know he understood that.

She taped a note to his bathroom mirror and one on his pillow. They were more love quotes. One by Mandino about treasuring love above gold and wealth that she hoped would reach his heart. And one by Longfellow about love never being bought. She liked it because it reminded her that love was giving and she wanted to give to Preston.

She grabbed her cover-up, slid her feet into her sandals and headed up on deck. Preston stood at the back of the boat, leaning over the rail. The breeze ruffled his dark hair, and he seemed an island unto himself. She paused for a moment.

His lean, muscled body must draw women to him as much as his money, she thought. He wore a pair of trim black swimming trunks and despite the casual pose he seemed tense.

She hurried to him, her shoes clip-clopping on the deck. For a minute she felt like the awkward girl she'd always been in social situations, but then she felt the heat of Preston's gaze and slowed her stride. He made her feel like a woman, and as she moved she was aware of the sway of her hips, the way the fabric of her cover-up slid open and closed over her chest as she moved.

He straightened and walked toward her. As usual,

confidence was in every motion he made. "Ready for that swim?"

"Yes," she said, slipping her cover-up down her shoulders and tossing it on a chair.

A long, low whistle broke the silence. She glanced over her shoulder at him.

"Do you like it?" she asked.

"Hell, yeah."

He pulled her close to him in a fierce hug. His mouth took hers as he pressed his erection against her. Oh, he more than liked the suit. A surge of female power rushed through her, and she realized she had been given a gift, this ability to affect Preston.

He pulled back abruptly. "Let's go for that swim before I forget the plans I've made for your first time."

Plans. That must include more of the trappings of romance. They'd eaten their strawberries and drunk champagne on the deck. Preston had fed them to her the way she imagined Roman demigods feeding their goddesses on Mount Olympus.

The romance of their relationship seemed important to him. "Are you okay with this being my first time?" she asked.

He raised one eyebrow in question.

"I mean, I know it makes you uncomfortable." She didn't want to have another solo orgasm. She wanted to experience all of Preston.

"As you pointed out, you are a big girl."

"Why do we have to wait?" she asked, ready to make love to him now. Even on the deck of this boat.

"Because you deserve soft candlelight and flowers—a romantic fantasy."

"What about you? What do you deserve?"

"Less than you are giving me," he said.

"I don't need the trappings of love," she said.

"No, you need the real thing."

"Don't you?" she asked. It was the first time he'd come even close to admitting love might exist.

"I need you, Lily," he said, tossing his sunglasses on her cover-up. He stepped down on the attached dock and dove cleanly into the water. He surfaced a few feet away but didn't say anything else.

He needed her.

What had it cost him to admit it? She knew he'd deny the sentiment behind those words if she pressed him on it. But he did care for her.

Lily dove in after him and let him tease her into playing games that were fun but light, when what she really wanted was to hold him close to her and assure him that he deserved everything she had to give.

"Close your eyes," Preston said. Lily, who'd been an enchanting temptress all night, did as she'd been asked. Unable to resist the creamy length of her back for another moment, Preston bent and dropped a kiss on the center of her spine. He was ready to explode.

Dinner had been a nice affair, but he couldn't remember what they'd eaten. Lily had smiled across the table from him all evening, making him feel as if he did indeed deserve her love.

Knowing that Lily had never made love to another man, he'd wanted to give her something special today. But all of the teasing touches and innocent activities had whipped him to frenzy. His control was hanging by a thread. Could he hold on?

"Pres?" she asked. Everyone else addressed him formally. Always had. He wasn't sure how she'd given him a nickname, but it made him feel special...part of her circle of intimates. He wanted that, but at the same time feared it. This gift Lily was giving him had strings she didn't even realize it had. But he didn't dwell on that tonight.

His bed lay on the other side of that teak door, and he longed to have Lily under him. "Right here, angel."

"Can I open my eyes?"

"Not yet."

He opened the door to the master stateroom and led her inside. "Take off your shoes."

"Just my shoes."

"Any other articles of clothing you want to remove are fine with me."

She laughed. But she sounded nervous. Scrupulously she kept her eyes closed as she stepped out of her high-heeled sandals. She teetered for a moment, and Preston stepped forward to support her.

"Thanks," she said, her voice soft.

Preston led her forward. The carpet had been sprinkled with rose petals. He'd kicked off his own shoes. The petals were soft but not as soft as Lily's skin.

"This feels nice," she said.

"Open your eyes."

The room had been made to look like a romantic lover's dream. Candles lit every surface, flowers were laid in between and her negligee had been placed on the bed.

"Oh, Preston."

He loved hearing his name on her lips. He pulled her back in his arms, unable to wait another second to touch her. She sighed and put one hand on his back, the other behind his head.

"Thank you for doing all of this."

"I know the romantic fantasy is important to you."

"How?"

He brushed his lips against hers. He didn't want to talk. She tasted like sin itself—sweet, hot and tempting. And like the sinner he was, he took her mouth in long, drugging kisses, convinced he could stop after one. But he couldn't.

She writhed against him. He slid his hands down her back. He took her bottom in his hands and brought her closer to his aching erection. He'd been hard for so long. He didn't think he could slow down.

She pushed his dinner jacket off his shoulders, and he let it drop to the floor. "If we don't slow down now…"

"I don't want to, Pres, make love to me."

"Yes," he said, lifting her in his arms and carrying her to the bed.

He settled her in the center and undressed himself quickly. Lily's breath caught as she looked at him naked for the first time. She looked a little hesitant when she saw the size of him.

"Trust me," he said.

"I do," she said.

"Will you take off your dress?" he asked. He was afraid to touch her. She slid her dress down her body and kicked it to the end of the bed. She lay in the center of his bed, where he'd wanted her for the longest time, clothed only in the skimpiest pair of red lace panties he'd ever seen and that toe ring.

The color inflamed him. He fell to the bed, his hands caressing her pale body, his mouth suckling her breast and his erection rubbing softly at her humid warmth through the layer of lace.

She moaned and grasped his shoulders. Her nails bit into his skin, but he scarcely noticed the sting. Levering himself up on his elbows, he slid his mouth down her body. She tasted as sweet as he'd known she would. Not just of the innocence she projected but of something more. Something that he'd never tasted before. Something so hard to identify that he gave up.

Her pretty round breasts begged for his attention. He caressed her nipples with his fingers, and they hardened under his touch. He couldn't wait any longer. Bending to her slim body, he suckled her.

She moaned again. A deep, husky sound that brought him even closer to the edge. He trailed his lips to her other breast and sucked her nipple deep into his mouth. She writhed on the bed and held his head to her body.

Arching up under him. He slid one arm behind her to hold her to him.

"Preston…"

He'd die hearing the sound of his name on her lips. He couldn't wait any longer. He lowered her to the bed and slid his hand down over her smooth, slightly curved stomach to the nest of red curls hidden beneath red lace. Never had anything enflamed him more.

She was warm and wet to his touch. Impatiently he shoved her panties down her legs. She kicked free of them. Preston reached for the condoms he'd put on the nightstand before dinner.

He sheathed himself, glancing up to find Lily staring at him. He wondered what she was thinking. She smiled at him. That sweet, innocent grin that made him want to protect her from the world and from himself. But not tonight. Not while fierce desire pumped through his veins and testosterone robbed him of the ability to be rational.

"Spread your legs, angel."

She blushed and separated her thighs by the smallest inch.

"Don't you want me?"

"More than I'd believed I could."

"Then make me feel welcome."

She opened her arms and her legs. "Come here, Preston."

He did. He slid into her tight body carefully because he didn't want to cause her pain. But she was so incredibly tight. He waited tensely for her to relax around him, then thrust slowly, gathering momentum only as she started to move with him. That toe ring of hers scraped along his thigh, bringing him closer to the edge. Then he heard her breath catch and felt her body tighten around him, and she was calling his name the way she had that night on his sofa.

His consciousness dimmed and he thrust heavily until release washed over him in waves. He held her close in the dim candlelight, rolling to his back and keeping her pressed to him, their bodies still joined. He held her tightly and hoped she didn't feel the desperation pouring through him. Hoped she didn't realize how deeply into his skin she'd crawled. Hoped he wouldn't hurt her too much when he pushed her away, because he knew if he didn't she would leave on her own, and he'd only just realized how much that would hurt.

Ten

Lily had never experienced anything like what she'd shared with Preston. He was quiet but held her fiercely to him, and it worried her that he hadn't said anything. Was he trying to pretend she was just another woman? Like that blond society woman she'd seen him pictured with in New York.

Her soul insisted that the emotions she felt for him were too strong not to be reciprocated, but her mind wasn't as easy to convince.

He'd challenged her to convince him to love, promised her her heart's desire, and she'd only just realized those two were intertwined. That she would never have one without the other.

Preston shifted her to his side and left the bed for a

minute to dispose of his condom. Her thighs ached a little from accommodating him but she found she wanted him again. The fierce ache started at her center and spread outward.

"You okay?" he asked as he settled back into bed and tugged her close again.

"Yes. It was wonderful for me."

"Me, too," he said, his words special to her because he so rarely revealed what he was feeling.

"Did you get my notes earlier?" she asked, unsure of herself for the first time with him. From the moment they'd met he'd made her uneasy, but not like this. She'd always been sure of herself—that she could handle the situation and being in bed with him. Her body still dewy from his possession made her...uncertain. She remembered that love was giving.

"The one on the pillow?"

"Yes."

"You think love lasts longer than gold?"

"You know I do."

"That didn't convince me."

"There are so many poor people who are happy and love each other," she said.

"The fact that they have someone to share their pitiful existence probably creates that feeling of affection."

"Preston."

"Lily."

She knew that he was a tough, cynical man, but sometimes he made her want to scream. This love dare was taking everything she had to give, and Preston wasn't even close to acknowledging real love might exist in the world much less in his life.

"Let's forget about love for tonight and concentrate on each other. I've wanted you for so long."

"Me, too," she said, softly.

Preston pulled her closer to him. Silence built between them as he rubbed her back from neck to backside. She squirmed closer to him. He smiled down at her, that wicked seducer's grin, and she pinched his side.

"Stop teasing me."

He caressed her again, this time a deeper touch that furrowed between her legs to her feminine flesh, still sensitive from his earlier possession.

"I'm teasing myself," he said.

"Well then, I might do some of the same." Preston needed a lover who was bold. Someone who wouldn't cower and be afraid of him. She could be that woman. She was that woman.

"I'd welcome it."

She walked her fingers along the line of dark hair that tapered over his chest and stomach. It was springy and warm and smelled faintly musky. She leaned closer, wanting to taste him. She'd been so passive when they'd made love. She'd been unsure of what she was feeling and afraid to explore. But now, in the dim glow of the flickering candles, she wanted to know Preston.

"Can I kiss you?"

He nodded.

Leaning forward she dropped a soft kiss on his hard stomach. He sucked in his breath, and she used the edge of her teeth to trace the line her fingers had just followed. His manhood stirred. She tilted her head and glanced up his body at him.

"You like that?" she asked.

"Just a little."

"Want some more?"

"Only what you're comfortable with."

"You make me feel very sensual, Pres."

He watched her. His gray eyes hard as diamonds, but she thought she saw a sparkle there that hadn't been present before. "Show me."

She bit her lip. This was what she'd wanted. "I will."

She'd show him more than physical attraction, more than what they'd experienced earlier—she'd show him love. She caressed his chest. His pecs were hard and flexed when he moved his hands to lift her over him.

His erection pressed urgently against her thigh, and she felt control slipping further and further from her grasp.

"No more touching, Pres."

"You've got to be kidding, angel."

"I'm not. This time I'm calling the shots."

"You're in the driver's seat."

"Yeah, but it's a remote control car."

He laughed and she felt it everywhere they touched.

He hugged her close and kissed her hard on the lips. It took her a moment to realize he wasn't touching her.

She started at his head, traced the shape of his ear and bit on the lobe. His neck smelled of the expensive cologne he wore, and she burrowed nearer to him. She touched her tongue to the pulse she could see beating in his neck and watched his Adam's apple bob as the center of her body brushed over his erection.

She did it again and this time he tensed and sucked in his breath. She couldn't wait much longer to feel him inside her again. To feel him filling her where she'd always been empty. To feel she'd come home when she'd been journeying for so long.

"Can we make love again?" she asked.

He grunted.

She grabbed a condom from the box by the bed and slid down, resting on his thighs. She tore open the package and covered him with it. He gritted his teeth, his breath hissing out. "Come here, angel."

"I'm still in charge."

"I know."

She slid over his body and decided being in charge wasn't what she wanted. She didn't think she could impale herself on him. Wasn't sure how to proceed, and that disappointed her. She wanted to be Preston's equal, but—

"Lily?"

She nodded. He positioned her over his erection and thrust upward while driving her hips down. It seemed as though he went deeper than before. Her head fell back and she moaned. She rode him harder until she felt that unique feeling begin again deep inside her. Preston's hips moved faster and as her body tightened and lights swirled behind her eyelids he called her name and ground his hips against hers.

She'd never felt anything half as real as what she'd shared with Preston and knew he'd have to acknowledge that love had begun to grow between them.

The tickling of feminine fingers walking along his spine brought Preston out of sleep. He'd been enjoying a vision of himself on an island with just one other person, no phones, no faxes, no demanding meetings. Only two naked bodies on sugar-fine sand with a warm tropical breeze blowing over them with the waves nearby.

''Wake up, sleepyhead,'' Lily said in his ear. Her soft voice brushed over senses already aroused. Gentle biting kisses dotted his neck. Heat shot to his groin, and he started to reach for her but stopped. Lily would be sore this morning.

He knew that they shouldn't make love this morning. She hadn't protested when he'd rolled her beneath him in the early morning hours and taken her again, but he knew that accepting him had been painful for her at first before passion swept through her and brought her to completion.

He had never been a woman's first lover before. But it had felt right to be Lily's. There was an odd possessiveness running through him as if he had branded her in some way that made her his for all time. It was ridiculous, of course. He was a man who always moved on, but for the first time the thought of other men touching what had been his was unacceptable. He had to find a way to bind her to him. Sex was great for creating intimacy, but this morning he'd have to find another way.

"You're not one of those cheerful morning people are you?"

"Only when the morning is this glorious."

He smiled. Lily enchanted him in a way that made him want to believe in love, or at least tell her he did, but he never lied. He'd been on the receiving end of one too many "good-natured" white lies to ever do that to anyone.

"I'm almost tempted to open my eyes."

"What would lure you, Pres?"

You, he thought, but didn't say it out loud. Instead he rolled to his side and captured the fingers that had been caressing him. Her eyes were deep and serious, filled with the emotions she hadn't learned to hide, and it made him ache for her. She believed in love, and he'd bet his newest hotel she believed herself in love with him.

The unacknowledged part of his soul hungered for affection from her. Wanted to hear some avowal of her feelings for him, but the other part, the weary man who'd been left time and again, knew they wouldn't come. Not without a price tag.

He'd pay the price for Lily and not regret the money.

Though he'd be disappointed if she asked him for jewels or real estate, at least he'd be able to deal with her. Instead she came to him with her sweet innocence and sultry passion. Setting his body on fire and making his soul long for something his mind had proof didn't exist.

Time to get out of the bedroom and back to the real world. Back to a place where he could think on his feet and find some workable answers. In bed with Lily he was enticed into believing the fantasy—that love existed for him. "I'd get out of bed for breakfast."

She snaked her hand down under the covers to his stomach. He remembered her mouth on that same spot last night. Maybe they wouldn't be getting out of bed today. There were many ways to make love.

"I knew Grandmother was right when she said the way to a man's heart was through his stomach."

Though he knew she'd been teasing, her words put a damper on his ardor. *His heart.* The muscle had been beating strongly for years but she wanted to reach his other heart. The seat of his soul where all of his vulnerabilities lay.

He wasn't happy about admitting even to himself that part existed. He wasn't about to let Lily find it. He wasn't about to parade out all of his foibles even for Lily. "Is that what you are trying to reach?"

She glanced away, a pink blush spreading up her cheeks. His erection stirred beneath the sheets; he was too damned old to be ruled by his groin.

"I'll settle for whatever I can get from you, Preston."

"What if all I offer is passion?" he demanded. He'd been foolish to think that sleeping with Lily would be the answer to the questions plaguing him. Though he now knew how exquisitely they fitted together he still had no idea how to relate to her.

She bit her lip. "I'll take it but I want more."

"I don't have *more*."

"I don't know where we stand now."

He didn't, either. But he was the experienced one, and for once he thought he might have the upper hand with Lily. "We're having an affair."

"For how long?"

"However long it lasts."

"And if that isn't enough."

"It will be," he said.

She left the bed, picking up his shirt from the floor and slipping it on. She looked lost and alone. He regretted his honesty but wouldn't take back the words. She'd get bored with him. There was a big empty hole inside of him that couldn't be filled, and though he was content with that emptiness, he knew from the past that women weren't.

He watched her go into the bathroom, listened to the sounds of her shower, knew he had to get up. He entered the bathroom and gathered his shaving gear, preparing to use one of the other staterooms.

But he'd been alone all of his life and would be alone again, he knew. For a few more weeks or months, whatever time Lily had to spend with him, he wanted to wallow in the sunlight she'd brought to his life. He couldn't do that on his own. He couldn't do that in another stateroom. He could only do that with her.

He entered the shower. Lily's eyes widened as he stepped inside, and for a moment he was afraid she wouldn't come into his arms, but as he spread them wide she didn't hesitate. He held her with a desperation he hoped she wouldn't notice and then loved her as if she was the only woman on the planet, and for a while he believed she was.

Lily tried to hurry through the cleaning of an eighteenth-century chandelier but she knew that a quality job took time. She should have finished the chandelier two weeks ago, but she'd been spending every free minute with Preston. Although his schedule was much more demanding than hers, she knew she couldn't keep giving unconditionally.

A glance at the clock told her it was time to wrap up for the night. It was November 1, All Saints' Day, and she'd visited her parents' gravesites that morning to deck the tombs with flowers. Tonight she'd convinced Preston to visit one of the candlelight vigils held in one of the older cemeteries in the city.

Already night was beginning to fall and the sounds from the French Quarter beckoned. She grabbed one of Dash's jackets and headed outside to wait for Preston. November had a chill that made her long for the humidity of September.

Last night for Halloween she'd asked Pres to dress as a vampire and help her hand out candy to the local kids at the school gym, knowing this would be a first for him. He'd agreed without any hesitation and had donated electronic toys for each of the seven hundred children who'd preregistered. Preston had made her agree to play Lady Godiva alone for him in her house after they'd returned home. Remembering his passion made her smile.

There was more to the arrogant person Preston wanted the world to see. Slowly he was letting his guard down, and each new layer he revealed made her love him more. She was working on the love dare and felt as if she was getting close to a breakthrough. He no longer seemed so distant and often prompted her for the quote of the day.

He'd even surprised her by spending an evening on her front porch wrapped in her arms while he read her poetry from Lord Byron. His warm, dark voice swirled through her mind. With a few nudges Preston could be a very romantic person.

He pulled up in his fancy car and called to her from the open window.

"Lily, you ready?"

She walked to the car and got in. The sounds of the Dave Matthews Band filled the air. She loved the jazz band and had given Preston one of their CDs. He'd gone out and bought every CD the band had made and tried to give them to her. Uncomfortable accepting presents, especially from him, she'd returned them.

Slowly all of them were ending up at her house or in her possession by default.

"Have you heard this one? It's another live album."

"It's good."

"I'm sure we won't be able to listen to the whole thing tonight. Metarie Cemetery is only a short drive across the city. You can take it home with you tonight."

"I'm not taking the CD, but I'll take you."

"Not unless I take you first."

He leaned over for a quick, thorough kiss that left her feeling branded. He glanced over his shoulder and pulled out onto the street and headed for the cemetery. All Saints' Day was celebrated in unique fashion in the Crescent City. She'd been going to the evening celebrations since she was a little girl and still cried when she remembered the first of November, the year her parents' died.

"Looking forward to tonight?" she asked, as he finally found a place to park the car.

"I have to admit it creeps me out."

"A little?"

"A lot," he said with a laugh.

A group of people passed them with flowers in their hands. Preston tugged her close to his side, slinging his arm around her shoulder.

She'd brought chrysanthemums earlier to her parents' sites. And she wondered if Preston had anyone to remember. He spoke of his father as if the man were dead, but she really knew nothing of his family.

They'd entered the cemetery, which used to be a racetrack way back in the late 1800s before being converted to a graveyard. Slowly they walked hand in hand through the candlelit plots, pausing to read inscriptions and listening to the conversations of those keeping vigil.

"I've always used this time of year to remember people I've lost, regardless of whether they're buried in New Orleans or not."

"Who are you remembering this year?" he asked quietly.

"My friends Pam and Carol." She still saw their smiling faces and remembered the good times with them. It was kind of cleansing to share her memories of them with Preston. She talked about them for a few minutes, knowing they would have liked Preston.

"Who are you remembering?" she asked.

"This is your tradition not mine."

"Have you lost anyone close to you?" she asked. She knew he was uncomfortable with the topic, but she wanted to know more of his past. Never had she met anyone who ignored it the way he did.

"I don't think I have."

"What about your parents? Your dad's dead, isn't he?"

"Yes. My mother is, too. But we were never close."

She started to ask another question but he placed his fingers over her lips so softly. She looked into those gray-lake eyes of his and for once they didn't seem frozen. "Have I told you how lovely you are tonight?"

She shook her head, letting him change the topic she so desperately wanted to pursue. She knew the key to teaching him to love was in the past but she'd yet to find it.

"Well, you are exquisite."

"Oh, Preston, you say the silliest things."

"I don't."

But he did. She was an average, ordinary girl—the girl next door—and he always made her feel like a fairy princess. Even tonight, surrounded by the crowds at Metarie, she felt like the only woman in the world beautiful enough for him. She was ready to go home with him. To reaffirm the bond that she knew was growing between them. To make love with the man who'd taken over her heart.

"I have one more thing to show you, then let's go home."

"Let's hurry."

She led him to a rather plain-looking tomb. The flickering candlelight made it hard to see the inscription, but Lily had tucked a small flashlight into her jacket pocket before leaving her shop.

The words were simple. A large tomb that held the bodies of...

Two Lovers United on Earth, Together for Eternity.

"What do you think?" she said, sniffing a little at the injustice of a couple dying when they were only twenty and twenty-two.

"That you are one in a million."

Lily knew then that a real chink had opened in Preston's armor. Loving him was bringing him closer to her, and she wouldn't stop until he could see what she'd only just realized. They were a couple for all time. With that magical love that would outlast time.

Eleven

Preston had made two trips to the office, even though it was Thanksgiving. When he returned the second time, he found himself surrounded by Lily's family.

Mae, her assistant, and Jim, Mae's husband, had arrived with a store-bought pie and a bottle of domestic wine. Her neighbors, the Conroys, a golden anniversary couple, had arrived next. Preston had found himself seated on the couch next to Mr. Conroy, listening to tales of his courtship of Annabelle and how he'd convinced her to marry him.

Lily's family was a little intimidating. They were all so protective of her that he felt uncomfortable. Like the cold seducer he'd started out being. He couldn't explain to them what he didn't understand, but he knew that Lily meant more to him than only nights of pleasure.

He felt like a heartless Casanova who'd coaxed their little lamb out into the cold, dark world and taken advantage of her. Even though he knew Lily had come to him of her own free will.

Business was the one thing he could count on. The closer Lily got to him the faster he wanted to retreat. She'd refused to let him sleep over last night with her brothers at home. She didn't want to give them the wrong impression.

He didn't have the heart to tell her that they weren't fooling anyone. Dash and Beau knew he was more to their sister than a business associate. Her grandmother, a young-looking sixty-eight-year-old, had waved her arms around him and read his aura.

She'd stared into his eyes and muttered something in a language he couldn't recognize.

"You've got potential," she said before walking away.

It had been a bit of a weird experience, and Preston would take on both of the brothers with one arm tied behind his back before he allowed Lily's crazy grandmother to corner him again.

"Pres, would you give me a hand in the kitchen, carving the turkey?"

He followed her down the short hallway, aware of Dash glaring daggers in his back the entire way. "You're not doing me any favors by alienating your brother."

"Don't be silly. Dash likes you."

"He'd like to see me staked out in the sun."

"I told him we were friends."

"Men aren't fooled by that old line."

"But they can be fooled into believing love exists."

"Lily…"

"I know. I'll leave it be. There's the bird. Do you know how to carve it? I saved a page from a magazine with the proper instructions."

"I've never done it before."

"Do you always eat out on the holidays?"

"Sometimes. But when I'm home, my cook takes care of this."

"Oh, should I go get Dash?" she asked. He knew she'd be disappointed if he said yes. And he didn't want to disappoint Lily.

"No, I'll do it."

It felt strange but also right to be carving the turkey. An image danced through his mind's eye of Lily and him and a brood of kids filling the kitchen. He blinked. He wasn't a family man, dammit.

He finished cutting the bird per the instructions. Lily slid up behind him and gave him a kiss on the cheek. He wanted more. He wished her family and friends were somewhere else so that he could take Lily here, in the kitchen, with the savory smells filling the air.

"Good job," she said.

He bent and took her mouth in the kiss he'd been craving since he'd been banished last night. "I can do better."

"Pres, we have a houseful of people."

"They wouldn't miss me."

"I think Humberto would."

Preston had talked briefly with Lily's grandmother's husband. He was an interesting man who'd been an investment banker for thirty years.

"Your brothers wouldn't," he said wryly. There was something unnerving about the two intense young men who'd been tag-teaming him. Asking discreetly about his intentions and promising retribution if he made Lily cry. It had made him realize that he didn't want to ever make her cry.

"I'm sorry."

"Don't be. You're their pretty sister, and they're worried about you."

She blushed at the compliment and stood on her tiptoes to brush a kiss against his jaw. Desire tingled to life, and his pulse beat heavier.

"It's because they love me."

"Not today, Lily. Please don't start on *love* today." Especially not while he held her in his arms. She felt small and vulnerable, though he knew she took strength from having those she cared about around her.

"Why not?"

Preston felt his pager vibrate at his waist. Saved by the bell, he thought. He let go of Lily to read his alpha page.

"What's up?" she asked.

"I just got paged," he said, reaching for his cell phone. *Thank God.* He'd had enough of hearing about happily ever after and how he'd better treat Lily right. He needed a break. But Lily was staring up at him with those beautiful blue eyes of hers, and he knew he wouldn't leave if she asked him to stay.

"On Thanksgiving? That's ridiculous."

"The resort industry is busy on holidays." Which was true.

"Is there a problem at one of your domestic resorts?"

He shook his head. "I like to have the general managers to call me every two hours with updates. I'll just go out to my car and make the calls."

"Preston, you're not leaving again."

"Why not?" he asked. He knew what a caged animal felt like, because he was trapped and walls were closing in.

"It's Thanksgiving. You don't have to return calls."

"Lily, I have to—"

"Please, Preston."

She'd never really asked him for anything before and he knew he couldn't tell her no. He nodded because he felt raw and aching, realizing for the first time what had been missing all of his life. He knew that there was no way he could make it last. Knew there was no price he could pay to convince Lily to leave this all behind and travel with him throughout the world.

Lily wrapped her arms around him and held him tightly. His own arms hung limply by his sides. Fear swamped him, and he was afraid to touch her. Afraid to reach out because she might disappear. Afraid to

KATHERINE GARBERA   155

trust in the dream he'd only just realized he'd been searching for all his life.

He was startled to understand that he wouldn't mind staying here. That he would gladly give up the hotels and traveling, the excitement of being a mover and shaker in the hotel industry, if he could be guaranteed a lifetime with Lily.

But he also knew he wouldn't take the chance. Wouldn't risk what he knew couldn't come true. What Lily had never understood was that he knew life held no happy endings for spoiled rich boys who'd grown into cold men.

The thousand-year-old oaks that lined the driveway to White Willow House were creepy in the dark, Lily thought as she drove past them. The big circular drive that would welcome guests in just a few days was empty. Her old Chevy chugged to a halt in front of the Doric columns.

She'd miss this place once the job was completed. She wondered if Preston would still be in her life. A big part of her believed she'd made some progress in convincing him love existed, but another part knew he was a man who lived in the eternal present and always looked forward. He'd made a few vague references to his next resort in Barbados.

As sure as she'd been that she could convince him to love, it was hard to admit defeat. And most of the times it didn't feel as if she was losing the bet, losing the chance of a lifetime she'd been given. But other times her affection for him seemed doomed. Maybe it was the big oaks and weeping willows on the shoreline of his man-made lake that were influencing her feelings.

The landscape at White Willow House harkened back to the days of arranged marriages and illicit trysts between quadroons and upper-crust gentlemen. Though not a true Creole, she felt like one in her blood, and she wondered if her commoner status affected Preston's ability to love her.

A security guard rapped on her window, startling Lily into movement. Enough of these thoughts.

"You okay, Ms. Stone?"

"Yes, Jeff. I could use a hand with the writing desk and George I chair in the back of the truck."

"I'll help. I'm afraid most everyone has gone home for the night."

"I think we can handle it. I'm stronger than I look."

That's right, she thought. She was stronger than she looked. Strong enough to make even the hardest heart crack open and believe in love.

With Jeff's help she got the George I writing bureau to the owner's suite and situated. Jeff left her alone in the suite of rooms she'd created for Preston's personal use. The resort would have its grand opening on New Year's Eve only ten days from now. Tickets had been sold out for weeks and Preston had asked Lily to spend the night in the suite she'd created just for him.

In the weeks since Thanksgiving they'd grown closer and she knew he'd begun to need her the way she needed him. Loving Pres was hard. But worth the effort. He was coming to appreciate the little things in life and had stopped trying to buy her affections.

Still something was missing. She longed for the man she only barely glimpsed when they were alone in bed in the dark of night. The man who cradled her close to his body and whispered his plans for the future. The man who'd visited a graveyard at night and stood beside a century-old plot and held her like he was never going to let go. The man who'd been her first lover, and she had a feeling, would be her last. The man who'd conquered her body and soul.

"What are you still doing here?" Preston asked from the doorway.

"Working." Fatigue lined his face, and he moved stiffly into the room. As if he'd been sitting down all day. He worked too hard. Always trying to increase his revenue and outdo his competition.

"Are you ready to knock off?" he asked, rubbing the back of his neck with one hand.

"Sit down on the settee."

"Why?" He moved with ease through the room, and she congratulated herself on making him comfortable in the past. Something he'd never been before.

"I'm going to give you a neck rub."

"I'd rather have a naked skin massage."

"Not in your contract, bud."

"I'm willing to renegotiate."

"I'm listening." She wanted to renegotiate, as well. Wanted to be more to him than a lover. Maybe he was ready to admit that they could make a life together. A life as husband and wife.

"How does an all-expense paid trip to Barbados sound?"

"A vacation?"

"More like an extended stay. I've finalized the property deal and I'm ready to begin work. What do you think?"

"It sounds complicated." She'd love to travel to an island paradise with him, but she couldn't live there with him for the months it would take to open a resort.

"Only if you make it," he said, taking her hands and pulling her around to his lap.

She let herself rest against him, inhaling the clean, crisp scent of his cologne. It was easy to be lulled into believing that she and Preston were meant to be, when she sat close to him in the dark. But in her heart she knew that she couldn't travel with him as his mistress. Honestly, she wouldn't even follow him around the world as his wife.

Her life was in New Orleans with her shop on St. Charles Street and anything else would leave her feeling like a shell of a woman. She needed her family and her antiques and...Preston.

"Barbados is only complicated if you let it be."

"I can't go with you, Preston."

He was silent for a minute. Only the sounds of their breathing filled the air. She was afraid of what he'd say next. Of what his actions would be. Both of them needed something the other couldn't provide, and they were reaching the point where one of them would have to compromise. Lily didn't know if she could.

"Why are you here so late?"

"My boss is a slave driver."

"I'll have the man's job."

"You already do."

"Seriously, I was having a great fantasy of you in bed and me sneaking in and waking you up."

"What would this waking up involve?"

"Every nerve in your body."

"Ooo, I'm sorry I'm going to miss it."

"You won't. You'll just be lucid when we get started."

She smiled to herself. She'd given him a key to her house last week and he'd yet to use it. More than likely if she'd gone home he'd have woken her with the doorbell.

"I can't wait," she said, her heart heavy.

"You don't have to," he said. Picking her up in his arms, he carried her into the darkened bedroom and laid her on the bed.

Lily never seemed more out of reach to him than when she talked about love. He reinforced the bond he'd created between them by making love to her. Tonight he'd felt her slipping away. Knew that a woman like Lily wouldn't be content to travel around the world as his mistress, but he had nothing else to offer her.

She'd eschewed the things that women in the past had clung to. Even the trinkets that advertisers prom-

ised would please women didn't please Lily. She liked
roses and chocolates and fancy dinners, but he knew
she preferred quiet nights spent together in her home.

The navy-blue coverlet was plush. He wanted to see
Lily's skin against it. He'd purchased it with her in
mind.

The spill of light from the other room illuminated
the bed but also provided cover for him. He was torn
between wanting to see every nuance of Lily's face and
body as he made love to her and not wanting her to
see what he couldn't hide any longer. He needed her
with a quiet desperation that was making him doubt his
beliefs.

And she was slipping away. He had to keep her tied
to him. Had to find something to keep her close if only
for the next few days, until he left Louisiana. She
watched him with feminine awareness and something
else. Something deeper. He figured she'd been telling
herself that she was in love with him and when he
looked into those deep-blue eyes, he almost believed
she was.

He stripped off his clothing with impatient movements. Wanting to bond with Lily in the most elemental and satisfying way. Longing to feel her tender flesh
under his. To be held tight in her embrace.

Naked, he approached the bed. Lily had kicked her
shoes off and began disrobing as if sensing his urgency.
The primal animal that lurked beneath the surface of
his sophistication had been released. He had to bond
with her. Had to mate with her. Had to make her his.

"I can't wait," he said. His voice guttural to his own ears.

Lily didn't flinch away. Only opened her arms and welcomed him.

"Come to me," she said, her voice that of the sirens.

He took her mouth in a deep, drugging kiss. Her taste assuaged a thirst he wasn't conscious of having until she entered his life. He let his mouth leave hers and found the pulse at the base of her neck. Her life force flowed through his lips into his body.

He couldn't wait another minute to touch her. All of her.

He pushed her skirt to her waist and her panties down her legs. He palmed her breasts through the layer of her bra and shirt. Her nipples hardened and he needed to taste her. Not through a barrier of cloth but mouth to flesh.

"Open your blouse."

She followed his command. Her fingers working quickly on the buttons that lined the front of that white shirt. The one she wore when she had a meeting. The one she thought made her look professional but only made him want to peel it away.

Once her pretty breasts were bare, he bent and suckled her gently, knowing the kind of touch she liked. She writhed under him, and he took her nipple deeper in his mouth, scraping his teeth along her aroused flesh.

She was always so responsive. She made him feel like the only man in the world.

"I need you now, Preston."

The words sliced through him, fueling the desire already careening out of control in his veins. He couldn't wait a minute longer, had to make her his own. Sliding his hands up her thighs, he caressed the hidden secrets of her body. She was warm and wet.

He stretched her carefully open with two fingers and positioned himself at the portal of her body.

"Hurry, Pres."

He lifted her hips and slid home. She tightened around him and he plunged faster and deeper taking her into his soul. He reached between their bodies and stroked the center of her desire until she made that high keening sound that signaled her climax. Preston grabbed her hips and plunged one last time. The release spread throughout his body, and he let himself rest cradled in her arms.

Knowing he'd found the home he'd always searched for. Knowing he'd found a woman to match him on every level. Knowing he'd finally met the one woman who couldn't be bought.

Twelve

Lily had looked forward to the evening of the grand opening. She felt like Cinderella finally going to the ball. It had taken her two weeks of shopping, but she'd finally found a dress as magical as she hoped the evening would be. It was only a simple sheath, but it was made of a light-green, almost see-through, chiffon and covered in sequins and beads. She'd splurged and spent time in the tanning salon to make sure her back was tanned so that the deep vee in her dress wasn't wasted.

She'd had a pedicure and manicure and felt feminine from the top of her coifed hair to the tip of her painted toenails. Standing in front of the mirror in only her underpants and high heels she thought that later on Preston would enjoy what was underneath the sexy dress as much as the dress. She spritzed perfume on her body and then wiggled into her dress.

Her hair fell around her face in sassy curls and she applied just a little blue highlight to her eyelids. She wanted everything to be perfect tonight because she was going to present Preston with the perfect couple. The one he denied existed. A man and woman who were together for one reason and one reason alone—love.

She'd had her doubts that Preston would believe in love, but after Christmas morning when he'd held her tight and told her he never wanted to let go—the first time he'd ever come close to confessing what he was feeling—she'd known he loved her. He didn't have any practice saying the words or identifying the emotion but once he realized how perfect they were together, he'd understand.

She'd softened him up by writing another love quote in a card decorated with a picture of Bourbon Street in the rain. She wanted him to see it tonight before she confessed her love. She'd added candles around the room. And put her favorite Miles Davis CD in the player. Next to the quote she laid a specially wrapped gift she'd made for Preston.

He had everything money could buy so she'd thought long and hard to find something that he couldn't buy for himself. She'd decided on a collage on a red heart of their time together. A picture of the two of them at her cousin Marti's wedding was situated in the center, and around it she'd added the matchbook cover from Van Benthuysen-Elms Mansion where he'd first asked her about love. A post card from Rockefeller Center and a shell she'd collected when they'd spent their weekend together on his yacht. She'd added a bunch of other little mementos, but those held center stage.

She wanted Preston to see the love she'd showered on him. To realize how important they were together and how deeply their lives had become entwined.

Someone knocked on the bedroom door of the suite she'd decorated for Preston. She knew it had to be him. She took one last glance at herself in the mirror before crossing to let him in.

"Hello, angel."

Preston was born to wear a tuxedo. He made her feel underdressed in her flashy eveningwear. It had something to do with the ease in which he moved. However, the intensity in his gaze assured her he didn't find her apparel offensive.

"Turn around," he ordered.

She pivoted slowly, feeling every inch a woman and proud of her female body. And when she felt the brush of his lips against her neck, she melted back against him. Only with Preston did she feel this complete.

"Gorgeous. Want to skip the party and stay here?"

"No. I spent a lot of money on this dress."

"It's a shame none of it went toward fabric."

"Ha."

He continued to watch her with an intensity she

found unnerving. Was the dress not right? "It's okay, isn't it?"

"What?"

"My dress."

"If it were any more okay, I'd spend the evening fighting off every man at the party, to keep them from trying to steal you away from me."

She smiled at him. Her heart melting. "No one could steal me from you."

A darkness entered his eyes. She knew he didn't believe that any emotion could last. Even lust ended. Success and the flush of victory were short-term. How could love last? she knew he was asking himself.

"I would fight to the death for you, Preston."

"Let's hope it doesn't come to that. We're not dressed for battle."

He turned them so they were reflected in the mirror. He was strong and solid behind her. The man of her dreams, the one she'd hadn't realized she'd been searching for until she found him.

"I feel like I'm a fairy princess."

"Tonight you are."

"What happens at midnight?" she asked, unable to help herself.

"The prince will fulfill your every desire."

"You already do."

"Well, tonight I have something important to ask you," he said, and led her out of the room.

Preston had decided to formalize his request for Lily to come and live with him in Barbados. He knew she'd never settle for a marriage to someone who couldn't love her. He'd tried to convince himself that lying about love would be okay, but it hadn't worked. Relationships based on falsehoods never survived. Even he knew that.

But he was convinced he could persuade her to become his companion. To call Lily a mistress would be a slur on her character and on what she meant to him. He watched her charm her way through the crowded ballroom as the clock came closer to midnight. Instead of jealousy a certain sense of pride flooded him.

She was the perfect balance to his personality even in a social setting. She was charming and friendly and knew details about the people who surrounded him that Preston had never bothered to learn.

He'd never noticed the distance he kept between himself and others until Lily had entered his life. He waved at some friends but didn't stop to chat. He wanted to spirit Lily away from the ball.

Even though he'd scheduled the gala to take place on New Year's Eve, he didn't want to be in the middle of the crowds at the beginning of the New Year. He wanted Lily to himself so he could ask her to spend the next year traveling and working with him. They could renew their agreement every year at midnight. He kind of fancied the idea, especially when Lily had made her reference to fairy tales.

He'd even had a diamond-slipper charm made for Lily to wear once she'd agreed. It was a trifle, but she wasn't the type who expected expensive jewels, clothes and cars.

He pushed his way through the throng of men surrounding her. She smiled when she saw him and reached for his hand as he approached. She never broke her attention to the man speaking, but she'd let Preston know she'd been aware of him.

He claimed her for a slow dance. Needing to feel her close to him. Closer than this public place would allow. He wanted to carry her from this place but he couldn't leave yet.

"Everything going smoothly?" she asked, her fingers toyed with the hair at the back of his neck. Heat surged through his body. He hardened in a rush as if he'd never known the paradise of taking Lily into his arms and loving her deep in the night.

He forced himself to answer her question. "Yes. Several of my colleagues have complimented the decor. I gave them your business address."

"Thanks. I did do a good job here."

She flushed. He'd noticed that she could accept a challenge with finesse but a compliment always knocked her off guard. And while he'd take any advantage he could get with this feisty woman, she should be more confident of herself and her skills.

"You're too modest."

"No one likes a braggart."

"It's not ego when you acknowledge the hard work involved."

"I don't see you strutting around the room."

"Would you like to?"

"Oh, yes. But only if we're alone."

"You think I should strut."

"Yes, I do."

An uncomfortable emotion flooded him, and he changed the subject. He didn't mind wanting Lily with a desire that made him want her by his side, but he couldn't admit to caring for her.

"This resort is going to be the crown jewel in the Dexter Resort Hotel chain."

"It will always be special to me."

He cleared his throat and looked away. He was uncomfortable for Lily when she let her heart show. He figured she thought she was in love with him. He knew she couldn't be. He'd given her nothing of value. A few trips and some trinkets, but she genuinely cared about him.

"Well my dress blended very well with this crowd."

"You were concerned about your dress?"

"A little, but I've had more offers than you'd care to know."

"Any of them indecent?"

"More than a few."

"Should I call anyone out?"

"No."

He would do it, he realized, for Lily. She stirred his blood in a primal way that made him react at the gut level. "Are you ready to leave?"

"Your party isn't over yet."

"Ours is just beginning."

He kissed her. She moaned deep in her throat and clutched at his shoulders. That primal scream echoed in his body, urging him to pull her close. To never let go of her until he was hilt deep inside her welcoming warmth and home.

Home.

He hadn't realized he'd been searching for it, but there it was. She offered him something no one else could. The chance to be who he really was without the pressure of worrying about the image.

A discreet cough interrupted them. Rohr stood a few steps away with his very pregnant wife. "Excuse me, sir."

He left Lily talking with Mrs. Rohr while he and Jay discussed a minor problem the kitchen was having. By the time he'd put out that emergency and found Lily they had five minutes until midnight.

"Come on," he said, none of his usual flair.

"Where are we going?"

"I told you I want to have our own party."

"Cinderella got to stay at the ball until the ninth stroke of midnight."

"I'll give you at least nine strokes at midnight."

She blushed but patted his backside. "I'll take you up on that."

He hurried her through the lobby and into the elevator, impatiently waiting until they reached the penthouse floor. He swept her up in his arms and carried her down the hallway. For the first time in his life he almost believed he'd found something that could last.

Someone who'd stay with him forever. And though he would never admit it, that scared him to the bottom of his soul.

The moon spilled in through the skylights, painting the room in shadows. The candles on the dresser that Preston had lit earlier had died down. Her body, though, was still flushed from Preston's lovemaking. Overcome with emotion, Lily brushed a kiss on his well-shaped mouth. Preston pulled her closer, sucking her bottom lip between his teeth and nibbling on her flesh.

She wanted him again. But she longed to have their relationship settled. She broke their kiss, and Preston kept her close to him in the intimate cocoon of their bed.

"What did you want to discuss with me?" she asked him when her breathing settled.

"I have an offer for you. Wait here." He padded naked through the room to his closet. She loved the way he looked naked. His hard body moved with ease and grace.

When he removed a small box from his coat, she grabbed her present, too. The one she'd made for him from her heart. He had a gift for her, she thought.

She turned on the nightstand lamp, wanting to be able to see his face when he realized he was in love with her. And she knew that it would probably shock him. He'd been resistant to emotions since they met but he'd changed since the night they'd visited the graveyard.

"I have something for you, too."

He sat next to her on the bed. He stared at her chest. Her nipples tightened. If they were going to talk, it had to be fast. She tugged the sheet up to cover her breasts.

"Talk fast, Lily."

She nodded. "This is harder than I thought it would be."

"You don't have to say anything."

"I do. You see, Preston, while I've been searching for true love and convincing you it existed... What I mean to say is I've found the perfect couple."

"Who are they?"

"Us."

"Us?"

"We're perfect for each other."

"Lily, listen, we're good in many ways, but that doesn't make what we have love."

"How would you know what love is?"

"I know what it isn't."

"Then why are we together?"

"Lust, money."

"I don't want your money."

"What do you want?"

"Your love. I love you. Those aren't words that I say lightly but I need you in my life."

"Lily, I'd like you to be part of my life. Things don't have to change."

"What do you mean?"

"I have a gift for you that will cheer you up."

She doubted it, but took the small jewelry box from him. Inside was a beautiful diamond pendant in the shape of Cinderella's slipper. It took her breath away and proved to her how well they knew each other. She felt like the struggling girl to his wealthy prince.

"I'd like you to be my companion for the next year."

His words made no sense to her. She suddenly realized that Preston wasn't thinking of happily ever after. "Companion?"

"Yes, travel with me and be my partner."

Oh, God. Her heart shattered in a million pieces while he continued speaking. Telling her the places they'd go. Barbados, again.

Preston saw a future for them that involved her running from the past, too. And she wasn't willing to do it. Wasn't willing to chuck a lifetime worth of memories for a man who thought that lust and money were the key ingredients to a successful relationship.

On shaking legs, she stood. Preston stopped talking, and she felt his gaze on her as she gathered her clothes. She was embarrassed by her nudity and hurried to put on her jeans and shirt. The damned buttons were crooked but she couldn't fix them now. She tossed her lovely dress into her garment bag and started putting her other things in there.

"Lily, where are you going?"

"I'm leaving."

"I don't have time for games. I have to be in Barbados on Monday."

Anger left her speechless for a moment. She was less important to him than his schedule.

"How can you be so stubborn? The truth is all around us."

He stood, but she couldn't look at him. Couldn't see the man who'd taught her the beauty of physical love and the pain of the emotional. "The truth is there is no perfect couple or perfect love."

"I know love isn't perfect. All I know is that I'm in love with you."

He put his arms around her. Cradled her in his warmth, rubbing her back and speaking gently in her ear. Tears burned the back of her eyes. She blinked frantically trying to stall them. "Calm down. Please don't leave like this."

She loved him, but not enough to give up her life and become what he hated. And she knew she would. He'd start giving her gifts instead of his time and because she'd spend her time alone waiting for him to return to her she'd take them. She pictured herself alone in a hotel room in a foreign country while Pres was off working.

"I can't stay. I've been telling myself that you can love. You see, I've loved you for a long time, and I know that love hurts. But you won't even admit you can be hurt by it."

"That's because—"

"Don't say it doesn't exist. You have to take a risk for love to come to you." She stalked away from him.

"The truth is, Lily, I know all about so-called love. I've heard those words before, and every time I wasn't willing to pay to keep that person around, love disappeared."

"I'm different."

"Prove it."

Ah, a ray of hope, she thought. "Open my gift."

He opened the card and read the quote inside. He didn't touch the wrapping on her heart. "I knew it."

His soft words should have elated her, but the expression on his face told her that he'd missed the point.

"'Love is a rain of diamonds in the mind,'" he said, softly.

"Did you understand why I left it?" she asked.

"Yes. I'm sorry but I don't have a shower of diamonds for you. If you open the box, we can consider this a deposit."

Lily searched the room for her purse. There was no way Preston was ever going to understand. He couldn't love her because he only understood one thing: money and the power it held over humanity. She blinked again trying to hold back her tears.

"Well, it looks like you've won our bet," she said.

"This wasn't about a bet."

"No, it wasn't. But it was a gamble all the same."

"Stop talking like you just lost big in Vegas. I'll shower you with diamonds."

"I'd rather be showered with your love."

He said nothing. She sniffled and knew that blinking wasn't going to stop the tears from falling. ''Goodbye Preston.''

She ran from the room as if the demons of hell were chasing her. But she knew they weren't. Her demon was all too real and more painful, because she knew that he didn't have to be a demon but chose to.

Thirteen

Preston picked up the jewelry box that Lily had discarded in her mad dash from the room. He called down to security and asked one of the guards to follow Lily home. To make sure she made it back to her place safely.

Uncomfortable with the feeling that he was alone again, he crossed the suite to the bar and poured himself a stiff drink. The alcohol bit as it went down, but he didn't flinch. Unnamed emotions roiled through him as he caught his own reflection in the mirror across the room. He looked like a man who'd lost everything.

He threw the glass against the wall and listened to it shatter. The suite felt too small and confining. Memories of Lily were everywhere. He saw her as she'd been just a few nights ago, standing at the window and looking at the darkened lawn. He saw her in her work-shop refinishing the settee that now graced one of the walls.

He remembered her face when she'd offered him a massage because he was tired and he'd seduced her into his bed once again. Knowing that he couldn't give her what she needed, he'd offered her only what he had.

And it wasn't enough.

He called the airport and had them ready his jet. He needed to get out of New Orleans. Away from the slow-beating rhythm of the South and the memories of Lily. She'd taught him to care again and then left him.

He walked into the bedroom to dress and caught sight of Lily's gift to him. He'd never opened it. Never looked at it to see what it was she'd given him. He'd been so focused on making her stay with him.

He would open it later. He packed his clothes and glanced around the suite one last time. Something glittered in the corner of the room. *Lily's shoe.* That pretty silver high-heeled shoe that she'd worn last night. The shoe that had made her feel like a princess and him like her fairy-tale prince.

When had the prince turned into a pumpkin? When had the clock struck twelve for them?

He placed her shoe in his briefcase next to the wrapped gift. He told himself it was so that he'd have something to remember her by, but he knew he'd never forget Lily.

He called downstairs to have his car brought around and walked out of the suite that had become more of a home to him than he'd ever had before. More of a home than he'd ever expected to have. He never looked back and didn't now as he walked away from the resort. But he wanted to. He wanted to glance over his shoulder and see in his mind's eye Lily standing in the doorway.

But he didn't.

It was chilly in the early-morning hours. The road was clear of traffic as late-night revelers slept off last night's celebrations. Preston tried to make sense of Lily's departure.

He still couldn't understand what she wanted from him. He'd promised her a life of excitement and riches for at least a year.

Maybe she wanted more than a year, he thought. Maybe she didn't care about the money. In retrospect it seemed as if he might have overreacted to her quote about diamonds. Normally if a woman walked out on him he wouldn't care, but he'd already acknowledged to himself that Lily was anything but normal in his life. He picked up his cell phone and dialed her home number.

It rang eight times.

"Hello."

Lily's voice sounded as if she was still crying. A strange pain assailed him, but he didn't examine it. *Angel, I never meant to hurt you.*

She sniffled but said nothing else. He hung up the

phone. Lily wasn't a woman who'd live with a man without the hope of family and lifelong commitment. He had no right to her sweetness and he knew it.

The silence in the car was deafening, and his own thoughts were making him crazy. He turned on the CD player and the sounds of Miles Davis filled the car. Lily had it cued to her favorite song, "I Thought about You."

He'd give himself tonight for the memories and then he was moving on. Lily Stone was a part of the past, and Preston Dexter never, never looked back.

New Orleans was gearing up for Mardi Gras, but Lily didn't feel like celebrating. She'd signed the contract to refurnish and redecorate an older mansion that a friend of Preston's had purchased. It had hurt to hear his name, but she was trying to move on. Falling out of love wasn't easy. In fact, it was really hard. Her brothers were planning a visit for Mardi Gras the first week in February and Lily knew she had to get over Preston before then.

She had to start sleeping again. She had to find a way to forget about the two of them on her love seat almost making love. She had to find a way to forget he'd ever shared her bed and then shared her kitchen with those soulful eyes of his that made her want to show him the world because for all his wealth Preston couldn't see it.

The cellular phone rang and she answered it. Nothing but silence on the other end.

"Hello?"

"Lily, its Jay Rohr. We're processing the final payment to you today and I wanted to thank you again for the wonderful job you did with White Willow House."

"Thanks for the opportunity, Jay. I learned a lot from the project." More than he'd ever know, she thought.

"Are you at your office, Lily?"

"No, I'm on my way home. Why?"

"I wanted to fax you the final change order for signature."

"Oh, I can swing by and get it."

"It can wait until morning if you're on your way home now," Jay said.

"I am."

She asked about his wife and their new baby, a girl they'd named Angela, and then she concluded the call. She wanted a baby of her own. She'd spent the day in the import yard, and she was tired. She'd found a piece that she knew Preston would love but had not purchased it because she was going to get over him.

Pulling into her driveway, she sat for a moment looking at the small Creole cottage that been her home all her life. She remembered her mom and dad dropping them off to stay with her grandmother while they went off to explore cultures of hunter-gatherer tribes around the globe. She remembered leaving in the black limo the day they'd buried her parents. Playing tag football on the front lawn with her brothers.

But as she looked at the house now, she realized that

hanging on to possessions wasn't going to bring those people back to her. She'd stayed put for so long, craving normalcy and routine and only now realized that she'd been letting life pass her by.

Preston had given her someone to love, but she'd never been brave enough to love him more than her home. More than this old house and Crescent City. She opened her door slowly. She wasn't going to get over Preston because they were meant to be together, and if she had to follow him around the world to prove she loved him for him and not his money she was going to do it.

"She's on her way home," Jay Rohr said.

"Thanks, Jay. I owe you one," Preston said, disconnecting the call.

It had taken him three weeks to open the gift from Lily. He'd been sure that it was a steel watch or gold pen. Some sort of trinket that was worth a lot of money. His heart had stopped when he'd uncovered the photo heart she'd given him.

He'd stood in the empty living room of his penthouse apartment. The one with no photos of his family or links to his past and realized that love had been staring him in the face all along. That love had been what had kept him in New Orleans long after he needed to stay there.

That love had been why he'd hidden behind long-ago learned behaviors instead of remembering what

Lily had shown him. That love was giving. How many times had he heard that and not understood.

Finally he did, and he only hoped it wasn't too late. He'd been waiting on her porch for almost four hours and it was getting late. He'd had Jay call her cell phone on some pretense of business, but he wanted Lily back where she belonged. Back in the place he'd foolishly kicked her out of. Because he knew now he couldn't live without Lily. Oh, he'd survive but his quality of life would be below poverty level.

He'd missed the slow rhythm of New Orleans, Lily's jazz music and her crawfish pie. He'd missed the simple evenings they'd spent together in her family home.

But most of all he'd missed Lily. He'd delegated the Barbados resort to one of his junior vice presidents when he understood that his heart was in New Orleans. The organ he didn't think he'd had before a sweet, sexy redhead had dared him to believe in love.

How was he going to convince her that he'd changed his mind? A car pulled into the driveway, and Lily sat behind the wheel for a minute before stepping out of the car.

She looked more beautiful to him than anything he'd ever seen before. His hands started shaking and his palms grew sweaty. Oh, God, he didn't know if he could do this. What if she had given up on him?

He stepped from the shadows of her porch. "Lily?"

She froze.

For once he had no words. No glib comment or challenging dare. He had only his heart and he knew he wore it on his sleeve.

Carefully she crossed to him. The stadium jacket she wore was too big, and she seemed to have lost weight since he'd seen her last. He hoped to God she wasn't sick.

When she was an arm's length away, Preston pulled her close for a hug. Her curves fitted his body in all the remembered places. Damn, she felt good.

"I know you deserve better than me, Lily, but I can't let you go. And I want to get married and raise children with you and spend the rest of our days challenging each other."

"Why, Preston?"

"Don't you know?"

"I need the words."

He took a deep breath. "I love you, Lily."

She stared into his eyes. The only other time he'd ever uttered those words he'd lost the most important person in his life. Suddenly tears ran down her face and she hugged him to her tightly.

"I thought I lost you," she said.

"I thought you did, too."

"You're sure about this?" she asked.

"Yes, I am."

"When do we leave for Barbados?"

"We're not going. I don't have to oversee the opening of each new resort. I will have to go to the grand opening celebrations but I don't have to be so hands-on."

"Won't you miss it? I don't want you to regret being with me."

"I suspect that you'll keep me busy."

"Where will we live?"

"I'd like to divide our time between New Orleans and New York."

"That would work. I can take on fewer decorating jobs and just do refinishing work."

"We can talk about the details later," he said. "I have something for you."

He pulled her shoe from his pocket and got down on one knee. He took her left hand in his and brushed a kiss across her knuckles. "Lily Stone, will you marry me?"

Lily crouched down and kissed him. "You bet."

Preston stood and scooped her up in his arms, carrying her into the house to seal their love with lovemaking that put to rest the doubts of the past.

* * * * *

January 2002
THE REDEMPTION OF JEFFERSON CADE
#1411 by BJ James

Don't miss the fifth book in BJ James' exciting miniseries featuring irresistible heroes from Belle Terre, South Carolina.

February 2002
THE PLAYBOY SHEIKH
#1417 by Alexandra Sellers

Alexandra Sellers continues her sensual miniseries about powerful sheikhs and the women they're destined to love.

March 2002
BILLIONAIRE BACHELORS: STONE
#1423 by Anne Marie Winston

Bestselling author Anne Marie Winston's Billionaire Bachelors prove they're not immune to the power of love.

MAN OF THE MONTH

Some men are made for lovin'—and you're sure to love these three upcoming men of the month!

Available at your favorite retail outlet.

Where love comes alive™

Visit Silhouette at www.eHarlequin.com

SDMOM02Q1

If you enjoyed what you just read,
then we've got an offer you can't resist!

Take 2 bestselling love stories FREE!
Plus get a FREE surprise gift!

///

Clip this page and mail it to Silhouette Reader Service™

IN U.S.A.	**IN CANADA**
3010 Walden Ave.	P.O. Box 609
P.O. Box 1867	Fort Erie, Ontario
Buffalo, N.Y. 14240-1867	L2A 5X3

YES! Please send me 2 free Silhouette Desire® novels and my free surprise gift. After receiving them, if I don't wish to receive anymore, I can return the shipping statement marked cancel. If I don't cancel, I will receive 6 brand-new novels every month, before they're available in stores! In the U.S.A., bill me at the bargain price of $3.34 plus 25¢ shipping and handling per book and applicable sales tax, if any*. In Canada, bill me at the bargain price of $3.74 plus 25¢ shipping and handling per book and applicable taxes**. That's the complete price and a savings of at least 10% off the cover prices—what a great deal! I understand that accepting the 2 free books and gift places me under no obligation ever to buy any books. I can always return a shipment and cancel at any time. Even if I never buy another book from Silhouette, the 2 free books and gift are mine to keep forever.

225 SEN DFNS
326 SEN DFNT

Name	(PLEASE PRINT)	
Address	Apt.#	
City	State/Prov.	Zip/Postal Code

* Terms and prices subject to change without notice. Sales tax applicable in N.Y.
** Canadian residents will be charged applicable provincial taxes and GST.
   All orders subject to approval. Offer limited to one per household and not valid to
   current Silhouette Desire® subscribers.
   ® are registered trademarks of Harlequin Enterprises Limited.

DES01   ©1998 Harlequin Enterprises Limited

Desire

Bestselling author
CAIT LONDON
**brings you another captivating book
in her unforgettable miniseries**

*One Western family finds the love that
legends—and little ones—are made of.*

Available in February 2002:
TALLCHIEF: THE HUNTER
Silhouette Desire #1419

Return to Tallchief Mountain as Adam Tallchief claims his
heritage and the woman he is destined to love. After twenty-
two years, Adam has come home to the family he didn't
know he has. But his old love and enemy, Jillian Green O'Malley,
is back, as well, and the passion that has always blazed
between them threatens to consume them both....

**"Cait London is an irresistible storyteller."
—*Romantic Times Magazine***

Available at your favorite retail outlet.

Where love comes alive™

Visit Silhouette at www.eHarlequin.com

SDTALL

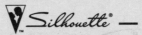

Silhouette® —

where love comes alive—online...

eHARLEQUIN.com

your romantic magazine

Indulgences

♥ Monthly guides to indulging yourself, such as:
  ★ Tub Time: A guide for bathing beauties
  ★ Magic Massages: A treat for tired feet

Horoscopes

♥ Find your daily Passionscope, weekly Lovescopes and Erotiscopes

♥ Try our compatibility game

Romantic Movies

♥ Read all the latest romantic movie reviews

Royal Romance

♥ Get the latest scoop on your favorite royal romances

Romantic Travel

♥ For the most romantic destinations, hotels and travel activities

All this and more available at
www.eHarlequin.com

SINTE1R2

You are invited to enter the exclusive, masculine world of the...

Silhouette Desire's powerful miniseries features five wealthy Texas bachelors—all members of the state's most prestigious club—who set out to uncover a traitor in their midst... and discover their true loves!

THE MILLIONAIRE'S PREGNANT BRIDE
by Dixie Browning
February 2002 (SD #1420)

HER LONE STAR PROTECTOR
by Peggy Moreland
March 2002 (SD #1426)

TALL, DARK...AND FRAMED?
by Cathleen Galitz
April 2002 (SD #1433)

THE PLAYBOY MEETS HIS MATCH
by Sara Orwig
May 2002 (SD #1438)

THE BACHELOR TAKES A WIFE
by Jackie Merritt
June 2002 (SD #1444)

Available at your favorite retail outlet.

Visit Silhouette at www.eHarlequin.com   SDTCC02

INTIMATE MOMENTS™
is proud to present

Romancing the Crown

With the help of their powerful allies,
the royal family of Montebello is determined
to find their missing heir. But the search for the
beloved prince is not without danger—or passion!

**This exciting twelve-book series begins in January and
continues throughout the year with these fabulous titles:**

Available at your favorite retail outlet.

Silhouette®
Where love comes alive™

Visit Silhouette at www.eHarlequin.com

SIMRC

Silhouette Books invites you to cherish
a captivating keepsake collection by

DIANA PALMER

They're rugged and lean…and the best-looking, sweetest-talking men in the Lone Star State! CALHOUN, JUSTIN and TYLER—the three mesmerizing cowboys who started the legend. Now they're back by popular demand in one classic volume—ready to lasso your heart!

You won't want to miss this treasured collection from international bestselling author Diana Palmer!

LONG, TALL Texans

CALHOUN, JUSTIN & TYLER
(On sale March 2002)

Available at your favorite retail outlet.

Where love comes alive™

Visit Silhouette at www.eHarlequin.com

PSLTT